I0788791

SHIFTED MAGIC

FATED TO THE WOLF – BOOK ONE

HEATHER RENEE

ISBN: 979-8423734695

Development Editing: Amy McNulty

Line Editing and Proofing: Jamie from Holmes Edits

Cover: Covers by Juan

Character Art Images: Samaiya Art

CONTENTS

DEDICATION

For Chanell Renea Drew.
Your light is missed in this world.

Beatrix's Coven
Spell House
os Angeles
Warlock
Vampire House
Holden's Pack
FATED
TO THE
WOLF
HEATHER RENEE

1

ANDIE

There was nothing like the sweet scent of denial. A lie I often told myself to feel better. In fact, there wasn't a single good thing about rejecting the truth. Stomach aches? Yes. Chest pains from increased anxiety? Definitely. An unknown, possibly magical, energy increasing inside me? Quite possibly.

Today was one of those days when the aches and pains were relentless. Even worse, over the last few months, each day seemed to get progressively worse. Yet, I hadn't figured out what any of it meant—just that the way I was feeling wasn't normal.

The bell jingled over the door to the gift shop I worked in, forcing me to shove my agonizing thoughts away and smile brightly at the new customer.

"Hello. Please, let me know if I can help you find anything," I called from behind the counter. I wasn't a pushy salesperson, but I had no problem chatting with the shoppers if that was what they wanted. Though, today I'd be okay if there weren't any other customers coming through the door before I closed up in six more hours.

A small smile played on my lips as I organized the gemstones on the counter to try to keep my mind from spiraling. The smooth moonstone I rotated in my hand reminded me of the necklace I'd been given on my ninth birthday that I kept safe in my jewelry box at home.

I'd been working at the gift shop ever since I traded the craziness of Los Angeles for a small tourist town in Montana after my mother died. I'd thought getting away from the big city life was what I'd wanted, but the longer I was here, the more my heart yearned, needing something more.

There was nothing wrong with the life I'd built out in the sticks, but I also knew something was missing. Only I had no idea what that something was.

The middle-aged woman with icy-blonde hair waved her hand in front of my face. "Excuse me."

I blinked rapidly. "Yes, I'm sorry. How can I help you?"

She pointed toward a section on the back wall. "Is the sale for only what's on that shelf or the whole wall?"

"The whole wall," I replied sweetly, using my "work voice" and feeling bad that I hadn't been paying close enough attention to the sole customer in the store like I was paid to do.

The woman's sage eyes widened with glee as she quickly went back to shopping. At least my boss was going to be happy. Speaking of, I could hear her footsteps coming down the stairs at a hurried pace.

"How was bookkeeping?" I asked when she came around the corner.

Madelyn's normally soft-blue eyes were red and puffy, and her olive skin was pale. "I'm so sorry, Andie, but I have to go. There was a death in the family, and I won't be back for a few days." Fresh tears fell down her cheeks, and she made a hiccupping sound.

Her grief hit me in the chest, and the floor felt like it was falling out from under me. Today was not the day for high emotions.

Madelyn sucked in a breath. "Oh, no. The order for the spring festival. It has to be done tomorrow, and I didn't finish the inventory."

She covered her face and began to sob. I took a few steps forward, pulling my boss into my arms with shaky hands as memories of my own sorrow rose to the surface. I'd experienced loss several times throughout my life, beginning with my father's death, followed by the disappearance of my aunt, then the passing of my mother a few years ago. The weight of being left behind time and time again had a way of staying with a person.

"It's okay. I'll take care of everything. Do you need a ride home?" I asked, putting on a brave face for her.

Madelyn shook her head, reminding me of my mom when she used to get frantic. "My husband Rob is coming to get me. It was my sister. There was an accident and… Oh, God. She can't really be gone."

I squeezed her tighter. "I'm so sorry, Madelyn. Don't worry about anything here. Susy and I will take care of whatever needs to be done."

She hiccupped again and pulled back to wipe her wet face with the sleeve of her cream-colored sweater. "Please, tell Susy for me. I just can't call her right now. I'll be back as soon as I'm able."

I was scheduled to have the next few days off, but if Susy needed the help with Madelyn gone, I didn't mind working extra shifts, especially under the circumstances. Maybe the distraction of more responsibility would be just what I needed, given I'd made no real friends since moving to Montana, something that may have been subconsciously intentional.

"I'll email you the inventory numbers and my recommendation for the order by the morning. Susy will be working tomorrow, but I can come in, too, if it gets busy. Everything will be fine here," I said confidently.

Madelyn nodded, but her eyes were vacant as her mind was likely focused only on the sorrow that she was feeling. "Thank you, Andie. I don't know what I'd do without you."

I saw her husband's car out front and guided her toward the door. "I'm happy I can help. I'll be thinking of your family. Again, I'm so sorry for your loss. Call me if you need anything."

Her shoulders shook, and she shuffled out of the door without another word.

After hearing of Madelyn's loss, my past was trying harder than normal to sneak its way to the forefront of my mind, but there was work to be done. So, I pushed the growing anguish to the recesses of my mind, where I tried to keep those kinds of feelings, then turned to the customer still in the store.

She stared sheepishly at me. "I'm sorry to bother you, but…"

I smiled at her, putting on my best customer service face. "Oh, you're not a bother. Let me help you with your items."

It was only noon, but after that interaction and the night of inventory ahead of me, I knew it was going to be one long-ass day.

While I walked to the counter with the customer's items,

tingles moved along my arms, causing familiar unease. Though, for the first time since they'd started happening, I didn't want to pretend the energy I could feel inside me wasn't there. Maybe it was time I stopped pushing everything down and figured out a way to move forward. Maybe it was time to find out if the magical stories my aunt used to tell me as a child had been more than fables to put me to sleep.

———

JUST OVER TEN HOURS LATER, I MADE A STOP IN THE BATHROOM before closing the gift shop. As I washed the dust from storage boxes off my hands, I stared at my azure eyes, taking in the permanent flush that graced my cheeks on my alabaster complexion.

I was okay. I'd made it through the day, and tomorrow would be the same. I just had to get home, put my newly pink hair in a messy bun, change into my favorite pajamas, and turn on the latest comedy show I'd been binging. A terribly lame night for most twenty-one-year-olds, but it suited me just fine.

I dried off my hands and headed toward the front door, glad that I'd been able to get the inventory done. I'd even stayed a little longer to email Madelyn the information she'd need for the upcoming festival just so I didn't have to wake up early tomorrow to do it. Hopefully, she'd have time to place the order on the website I didn't have access to. Otherwise, grief wasn't going to be her only problem in a few weeks.

My eyes burned from the longer-than-expected shift, and I locked the door behind me. It was dark outside when

I stepped onto the sidewalk. I let out a yawn, ready to be back at my small cottage house. Maybe once I'd had some time to decompress, I could start searching for my aunt again.

If the added energy and tingles were what I was beginning to finally believe they were, and Aunt Junie's stories had been real, I was going to need her more than ever. I didn't know why she'd left me, but hopefully by finding her I could get the answers I'd been longing for ever since.

A gust of wind blew over me, and I tightened my fleece jacket around me. It was mid-April, but in Montana, that didn't always mean warm spring weather. I'd done my best to grow accustomed to it after living in the woods for the last few years.

The businesses on our street were already closed, so it was darker than I was used to without their lights on, leaving only the dim streetlamps to guide my way. Though, it was the quiet that bothered me most.

My walk home usually only took ten minutes if I cut through the alleys, but an eeriness stirred inside me when I glanced up and down the empty street. The tension in my chest grew stronger than ever, causing my breath to come in ragged puffs.

Following my instincts, I turned left to take the main road. Even though it would double the time to get home, being out in the open loosened some of the unease plaguing me.

My hands warmed to an uncomfortable temperature as I swiftly walked toward home. My anxiety was spiking and causing an episode I wasn't prepared for. Normally, when they happened, I was safely tucked away in my house.

Tonight, I wasn't going to be as lucky if I didn't get my crap together.

I shoved my fists into the deep pockets of my jacket and picked up the pace, then began repeating my mantra inside my head.

Whatever was inside me was absolutely normal. If magic was real, it didn't have to be frightening. I wasn't losing my mind. Nothing about the pulsing energy dancing inside me was a sign that maybe I was just losing my mind. *Noth-ing.*

As my thoughts went rampant, the air around me cooled, making my muscles tense up and my chest burn with the need to draw deep breaths that I wasn't currently capable of.

By the time I got to the main street, I was practically running, but I stopped abruptly when a shadow passed in front of me.

This could not be happening.

The town I'd chosen to disappear in was low on the crime scale and only had about five thousand people who lived here year-round. It was big enough that not everyone knew your business, but small enough that people were friendly and not filled with road rage. It was the kind of place where someone could forget their past and settle into the unknown.

I took a shaky breath and scanned the streets. There was nobody in front of me, and the warmth in my hands stopped spreading. A small thing to be thankful for. I continued forward, only to hear footfalls behind me. Any control I'd thought I had over my anxiety was shattered.

My body started to tremble and the energy inside me lit up like wildfire. The flesh on my palms tickled as if flames physically licked up my skin, even though I knew my hands were safely hidden away in my jacket.

I tried to gracefully glance behind me when I turned the corner, but due to the klutz gene I'd inherited from my mother, I ended up ramming my side into the brick wall and seeing nothing helpful as I stumbled, barely staying on my feet.

Smooth, Andie. Real smooth, I thought, rubbing the sore spot on my hip.

I straightened and quickened my pace, but with every step closer to home, my apprehension grew. My palms were sweaty, and my heartbeat was quickening. I was halfway to my house, but the feeling of dread consumed me once again.

I pulled out my phone from my pocket and opened the ride-share app that was really only helpful during tourist season, but if a driver was near enough, I'd just stay right where I was, under the dim streetlight, until someone could pick me up and take me right to my front door. Yeah, that was the best idea.

As I started typing in my information, my phone zapped me, then the screen went black. I held the power button down, trying to turn it back on, but there was nothing happening.

"What the hell?" I muttered to myself, trying not to freak out again.

I looked around, wondering if the footfalls I'd heard before meant that someone who, with any luck, wouldn't look like a serial killer was nearby and I could ask to borrow their phone.

Of course, I wasn't that fortunate. Someone was definitely close behind me, but she didn't scream friendly with her long, grey coat and dark hair shielding most of her face as she stiffly leaned against the nearest wall, acting like she didn't see me.

When I turned to continue toward home, a second stranger suddenly loomed in the shadows at the opposite end of the block. I was pretty sure this one was a man, based on the short hair I could see peeking out from under the hat he had tilted down over his face, but he was dressed in the same type of long coat, concealing his body, so maybe I was wrong.

I quickly reassessed my situation. I couldn't go back, but going forward didn't seem like the best idea, either, so I decided to cut across the street and see what the two lurkers did.

Double-checking the road was clear, I darted across, thankful I wasn't the type of woman to wear heels. Converse were the safest choice of footwear for someone prone to accidents.

As I stepped onto the sidewalk opposite from where I'd been, a woman who looked eerily familiar appeared in front of me. Almost as if she'd come out of nowhere.

She was tall, possibly close to six feet with the spike-heeled boots that she wore over denim-blue skinny jeans. She also had on a black leather jacket with a golden silk top underneath that matched her hair. Her appraising eyes were a light amber color with darker brown rings around them.

"Hello, Andie. I'm Charlie," she said. "You most likely don't remember me, but I need you to trust me. I'm a friend of Junie's." She looped her arm through mine, dragging me farther down the street.

I tried to jerk away, but her hold only tightened. "How do you know my aunt?" I demanded.

Panic rose inside me. I'd just been thinking about her and now some stranger was here saying she knew her. Something about that was too strange to be a coincidence.

"We don't have time for that conversation right now. I just want to make sure you get home safely." Her gaze avoided mine and she glanced around before urging us forward with more strength than I'd expected.

"Um, I can manage that on my own, but thanks." None of my internal warning bells were going off with Charlie's closeness, but I couldn't ignore the rise of emotions swirling inside me. Things hadn't been normal for longer than I cared to admit. I had to be careful who I trusted, even if it was with something as simple as getting me home.

Well, that was my thought until things escalated to a whole new level of insanity.

A flash of light flew toward us, and Charlie yanked on my arm, causing me to crash onto my knees. "What the…?" I started to snap at her, but the appearance of white, shimmering magic growing around her hands shut me right up.

"Just stay down, Andie," she ordered.

Maybe it wouldn't be so bad to listen to the possibly familiar stranger for a minute and see what happened. If Charlie really did know my dad's sister, I could get answers to the questions I'd been trying to avoid for the last few months.

Or maybe things were only about to get worse. I couldn't be sure either way, but as my hands began to warm to an uncomfortable temperature again, I had a feeling I didn't have much of a choice in the matter.

2

ANDIE

The air became increasingly cold around us, and my breath came out in visible puffs. I searched for the people who I'd been leery of before Charlie had arrived. Fortunately—or maybe not so much if they were merely in hiding—they were no longer anywhere I could see.

Warning bells began to go off around me, and I tried to pull away from Charlie while she seemed distracted with her glowing hands, a sight I tried to tell myself wasn't familiar to my subconscious or normal or real.

Except the longer I stared at her, the more warmth filled me. Warmth of understanding and family and home. Something I hadn't experienced in much too long.

Charlie looked back at me, and her eyes instantly softened. "I wish we weren't meeting like this, but everything is going to be okay, Andie."

Maybe my warning bells weren't directed toward her.

"What's going on?" I asked while once again looking for the lurkers who seemed to have vanished into thin air.

All I'd wanted was to go home and distract myself with mindless TV until I fell asleep in my comfy bed. Maybe I'd already fallen asleep and whatever was happening was nothing more than a bad dream.

Fat chance of that, my subconscious tittered.

Charlie's lips parted as if she were about to answer me, but then something that I couldn't hear must have caught her attention, because she raised a finger and turned away from me to scan the surrounding area again.

I moved from my bruised knees to my feet but stayed bent down behind Charlie. Another gust of wind passed over us, causing my skin to tingle with energy and my breathing to become harder. I closed my eyes, trying to focus and get a hold of myself, but it was as if something invisible pressed down on me, trying to suck the life from me.

"What is that?" I groaned when my head began to pound.

"Dark magic. Push back and it can't hurt you," Charlie said without looking at me.

"Dark magic? Push back? What does that even mean?" I snapped. The stress of whatever situation I'd landed myself in was making my irritation rise. I might believe magic existed inside of me, but that didn't mean I knew what the hell that actually meant or what to do with the energy.

Charlie sighed, reaching for my shoulder once her hand stopped glowing. "I'm sorry. I'd have thought you knew more, but none of us could find you after—" Her words cut off without warning.

"After what?" I asked as she tensed, peering behind me.

No answer came from Charlie. Instead, a force strong enough to knock me back on the ground slammed into us. This time I ended up on my ass, which didn't hurt as bad as

I'd expected, given that I'd already jammed my hip and bruised my knees all within the last ten minutes.

Charlie grunted, standing up and grabbing my hand without seeming fazed. "If you can't protect yourself, we're going to have to run to buy a little time."

She pulled me to my feet, and we picked up the pace, heading toward the alley. I wasn't sure that was a good idea, but given that Charlie seemed to know who—or what—was after us, I let her lead the way.

"Where's your house?" she asked.

"About five more blocks away."

"The address, Andie. I need to know where I'm going." She jerked us left, then right, and left again before shoving me forward. An explosion sounded behind us, and I glanced back. Where we'd been standing just seconds before was now nothing more than dark green smoke with swirls of black whipping around the cloud.

Charlie's hand covered my mouth. "Don't get sick, please."

Before I could question why she'd say that, the world blurred around us, and my stomach dropped like I was on the world's worst roller coaster. My knees gave out when my feet touched the ground again only a half-second later, but Charlie was prepared for that and had a hold on my arm, keeping me upright.

Once I had my bearings, I glanced around and realized we were a street away from mine. I had no idea how she'd done that for two reasons. One: I'd never given her my address. Two: teleportation wasn't supposed to be freaking real.

"Are we closer or farther away?" Charlie asked, repositioning me behind her before she moved her hands around in the air in front of us, causing more white swirls of magic to appear. This time, they had tendrils of yellow moving within the swirls.

"One more block," I answered with a bit of awe in my voice. The longer I watched her, the more my freak-out was diminishing. I became entranced with whatever she was doing, making me forget all the reasons I should have been running for my life.

At least, until she yelled in my face.

"Run, Andie!" she demanded, giving me a hard shove.

Something dark and shadowy flew over my head, and my heart rate spiked again. Without wasting another second, I did as Charlie commanded and didn't ask any other questions. When I scurried out of the alley, I caught sight of something mystical shooting from Charlie's outstretched arms and wrapping around the shadowy thing that had flown near my head just moments before.

Come on, feet. Don't fail me now, I chanted internally as I lengthened my stride.

With extra care, I sprinted toward home, hoping like hell that I wasn't going to trip and get taken by some crazy, shadowy person. Or at least I *hoped* they were technically a person.

Before I could let my thoughts be overrun with fear, I cut through Mrs. Pearson's yard, knowing she didn't have a fence around her property that was catty-corner from mine. The wet grass seeped through my Converse, but I kept running at full speed, dodging all of the flowerpots she had scattered about.

Though, no matter how careful I was, I still ended up face-first in the cold grass thanks to a black hose I hadn't seen in the dark. I rolled over, trying to make a quick recovery, but my situation didn't improve after I'd kicked the hose off me.

Dark mist moved around my legs, keeping them pinned together. The same man from the street—at least I assumed he was since I hadn't gotten that close of a look before—appeared above me, grinning as he tilted his hat up and revealed midnight eyes, a scar on his left cheek, and dark hair hidden within the shadows.

"Hello, Andie." His voice was deep with a slight accent I couldn't place.

His trench coat fell forward when he reached for me. Without hesitating, I grabbed both sides of the coat as tightly as I could and shoved him to the side. My legs might have been bound, but I could still bend them and attempt to fight back.

He reached for me, and his lanky, tawny fingers grasped my long, light-pink strands, yanking hard until my body was forced closer to him.

His dark eyes leered at me. "That wasn't a smart move, Andie. Now I'll have to show you what happens to witches who don't do as they're told."

He lifted me up by my hair, and I winced and yelped loudly as I tried to get my feet under me again. Grabbing my shoulders, he sent a wave of energy through my body that felt like that of an electric fence.

Holy crap, that was painful. Still, my instincts had me fighting back as soon as my body stopped seizing, displaying senses I hadn't even known I possessed.

My head slammed forward, right into his chin since he was a half-foot taller than me, and I shoved my hands into his chest, falling back onto my ass at the same time since I still couldn't separate my legs.

My palms broke my fall, but my wrists paid the price and agony shot up my arms. I rolled over, resting on my elbows for a moment, then pushed up onto my knees just in time to see Charlie appear in Mrs. Pearson's yard. The fact that my neighbor hadn't woken up yet with all this ruckus shocked the hell out of me.

Charlie's hand slammed into the stranger's chest, her palm connecting directly with the top of his ribcage. White and gold flashes of light with wisps of the shadowy mist flashed between them, making popping noises while small sparks flew toward the sky.

The guy had smoke rising around him, but he didn't seem capable of moving due to whatever Charlie was doing to him.

"You have no claim to her. She is part of our coven. If you come for her again, just remember, I don't give second chances." Charlie released the man, shoving him back several feet.

He stumbled, sneering at her and then me before he disappeared into thin air. Yeah, that wasn't normal. Once again, I had too many questions circling inside my mind, along with a truckload of panic, making all my internal alarms go off.

Charlie bent down behind me, lightly touching my shoulders. Before I could ask what she was doing, the binding around my legs was gone. I got to my feet in the next second, brushing the dirt and grass off me while assessing my aches and pains. "What the hell just happened?"

"That man and woman were hunters attempting to use you as their ticket into a coven they shouldn't want anything to do with. If they'd succeeded in taking you, it would have had a tsunami of an effect on our community," she said.

"Coven?" I'd only heard that word in fiction and from the whispered stories Aunt Junie had told to me on the nights she'd visited. Tales of witches and magic and a home unlike anything I'd ever known.

Witches. Magic. Coven. The episodes I'd been having. I was beginning to realize they were all connected, and much more problematic than I'd previously thought.

"You don't remember any of it, do you?" Charlie asked, a trace of pity in her words.

"Remember what? I'm still trying to process how the magic I was only beginning to believe I could use is more than parlor tricks. And what happened to the woman with the guy who was trying to kill me? Where did you come from and how did you know I was in danger?" I rapid-fired questions at her and did my best to ignore the heat in my hands that had begun to build up again.

"That *guy* wasn't trying to kill you, but he was trying to kidnap you. Something he would have succeeded at if you hadn't put up a fight. I admit, after realizing you didn't know how to use your magic, I'm impressed you fought back instead of letting the fear paralyze you." Charlie's tone wasn't condescending, but it wasn't super friendly, either. I wasn't sure what to make of her yet.

She wrapped her arm around my shoulders. "Come on. We need to get inside your house, call Beatrix, and then get you out of here as soon as possible."

I pulled out of her hold, paranoia igniting inside me. "You're not taking me anywhere. Where's Aunt Junie?"

Charlie grimaced, looking at anything but my face.

"What happened?" I demanded.

"She, um, died a few months ago. We tried to find you, but we couldn't until I got lucky today."

No. No. No. Aunt Junie couldn't have been gone. I hadn't seen her in over a decade, but knowing she'd been out in the world somewhere had always given me a sense of comfort that I wasn't completely alone. I'd thought I could find her again. I'd thought I had more time.

"I'm sorry, Andie. We've had every witch in our coven searching for you, but she hid you away too well and didn't leave instructions for us regarding you in the event of her passing."

Aunt Junie had hidden me? That couldn't have been possible. I'd *chosen* to come to Montana. To basically hide myself. Though, I'd never really understood why or from what. Something that should have been weird, but I'd been raised by a mother who'd done odd things all the time.

Had the answers I was beginning to see I needed been right there in front of me this whole time? Quite possibly, but I was going to find out for sure just as soon as my pulse stopped racing.

3

FOSTER

My wolf raced through trees, chasing the unknown. We'd been sent on a hunt for our mate months ago, yet she was nowhere to be found. I'd been ready to go back to our home weeks ago, but he was insistent we stay. I was beginning to think my wolf was losing his damn mind, something neither of us could afford.

My mind is perfectly intact. Yours might be something we want to evaluate, though. As for our mate, she's close, and we're going to find her soon, my wolf said through our mental connection.

'Close' and 'soon.' Two words you've been throwing around a lot lately, I grumbled, ignoring his attempt to rile me up.

I hadn't even wanted a mate. I'd fought my wolf, wanting to stay right where we'd been. In a pack that allowed me to be alone without being on my own. Our life had been just fine before our creator, the Moon Goddess, made an unexpected appearance and gave us a scent to chase, stating we'd find our mate if we followed.

Now, we were in a forest outside of Los Angeles. A city I hated with a dark passion. One that was loud and busy and filled with selfish humans who cared nothing for the world beyond themselves.

They're not all bad, my wolf said.

He was annoyingly positive while I was jaded. Neither of us had yet to convince the other that our outlook on life was better. At least our stubbornness was something we had in common.

We should go to the pack, he suggested, guiding us nearer to the local wolf territory.

I knew my wolf wanted a pack and a home we could be close to, but we'd had both of those already. Had them and watched them be ripped away from us. I couldn't go through that again. It was enough that he'd convinced me to find this mate of ours. Joining a pack that wouldn't allow me to do as I please was too much to ask for. Not after what we'd been through.

Holden, the alpha of the local pack, knew I was in the area thanks to a witch named Beatrix that I'd had a run-in with during my first week in L.A. She'd found me in the supernatural club called Warlock. I don't know why she'd thought my presence was any of her business, but she'd had no problem asserting herself into my personal space, something I hadn't forgotten and easily recalled.

"Who are you?" she said with an air of disgust.

"None of your damn business," I replied with matching annoyance.

"You don't belong to the local pack. Does the alpha know you're in his territory?" she asked, and I didn't miss the underlying threat.

"I won't be a problem, so there is no reason to tell him," I replied before taking a long drink of my beer, hoping she'd go away.

She scoffed. "You're a rogue wolf. I don't believe for one second that you're not going to be a problem."

I really had no desire to share my personal business, but more than that, I didn't want to deal with this witch any longer. Knowing mates were a sacred thing to most supernaturals, I decided to tell her the truth.

"I'm looking for my mate. Once I find her, I'll be gone."

Her lips thinned. "How do you know she's here?"

"I just do."

"Right. Well, I'll be keeping an eye on you, Wolf. I don't like strangers around here any more than the alpha wolf does."

I'd thought if I kept my head down that would be the last I'd see of the witch, but she had more than "kept an eye" on me. She not only involved the local alpha but had also tried to get me to go to a pack in Texas where I might be more "comfortable".

Only Beatrix had underestimated my wolf's want in finding our mate. When the woman from the Texas pack had shown her face, I lost control of him and shifted. Ever since then, I'd been mostly left alone. Though, with every passing day and the scent of our mate getting fainter, I was ready to move on.

Our mate will find us here. I know it, my wolf said, listening in on my thoughts.

I hated to admit it, but after all these weeks, a part of me hoped he was right.

The idea of having a mate terrified me, but the thought of leaving my mate unprotected, in a world that sought to destroy everything good in it, was unacceptable. My innate responsibility was stronger than my fear of letting people in again.

As our claws dug further into the forest floor, picking up speed, I let out a sorrowful howl. Releasing just the slightest amount of pain that I still held inside me helped keep us moving forward, but nothing would ever soothe the jagged edges of my heart.

Not even a mate?

Had I mentioned my wolf was annoyingly positive *and* persistent?

I ignored his question, and we raced through the forest toward the highest mountain top. It was our favorite place to think and watch for any signs of this supposed mate.

When we got to the top, Holden, the alpha wolf, was standing there with arms crossed, looking out over the city. He was older with fine wrinkles curving around the edges of his face. He had short, dark, reddish hair and light-green eyes that saw too much each time we were around him.

I shifted so we could talk, assuming that was why he was there. Energy rolled through my arms and legs, sending shivers down my spine as I pictured my golden skin, shoulder-length russet hair, the facial hair I was overdue on shaving, and my nearly six-and-a-half-foot height.

Soon enough, my ebony fur disappeared, replaced by my tattooed skin and the jeans and black T-shirt I'd been wearing previously.

Holden nodded at me. "Good run tonight?"

"Yep. Did something happen?" I asked, given he didn't often come out of his way to find me now that we had an agreement about me staying in his territory.

"Not that I know of. We just wanted to check on you. We

haven't seen you in a while. Beatrix said you've been in the city a lot more. I was surprised when I heard that."

He and I both.

As much as I disliked the nosy witch, there was something about Beatrix's coven that had my wolf curious and searching out one of her properties in town. Neither of us had understood why at first, but I was beginning to put the pieces together and wasn't thrilled about the conclusions I was drawing.

"We're still searching for our mate," I said.

"And you think you'll find her with the witches?" he asked with a raised brow.

Clearly, Holden and I had come to the same conclusions. I'd just been trying to deny the thoughts growing inside my mind. It was the only thing my wolf and I agreed on—to a point.

She might not be a witch. She could be a wolf that needs a witch's help, like the one we heard about from Texas, my wolf said.

I knew he wasn't fond of a witch potentially being our mate, given that meant he wouldn't have a she-wolf to run with, but we didn't get a choice in the matter. We got who the Moon Goddess deemed a perfect match for us, even when we didn't ask for anything of the sort.

"It's not impossible for my mate to be a witch. We're following our instincts for now," I finally said to Holden.

"You know, if that's the case, then people are going to be curious about the two of you," he replied.

"People like who? You?" I snarled, my mood diminishing quickly.

He held his hands up innocently. "I've only tried to help you, Foster. I know what happened to you before, and I—"

I cut him off with a deep growl. "You don't know anything about me. I don't need or want your help."

Holden was an experienced and patient alpha. He didn't act on emotion, and I had no real reason to snap at him, but he was trying too hard to help me. He didn't understand that I couldn't allow that. It was already too much to let in a potential mate. I couldn't join a pack like his. Not now or ever.

"I'm sorry for overstepping. I don't presume to understand how you're feeling, but I am sincere in my offer to help. Even if you don't want to join our pack, while you're in my territory, consider me an ally. If you want help finding this mate of yours, just say the word."

I knew I was being an asshole. I believed Holden's sincerity. I just didn't know how to get out of my own head.

"Thanks, but we're good," I said evenly.

"The new moon is soon. If your wolf wants to run with us, you're welcome to meet us in this forest," Holden added as he took a step away.

My wolf whimpered at the idea. We hadn't run with a pack in over a decade. I'd stolen that from him in my need to keep other wolves at a distance. As much as I wanted to give my wolf this one night with a pack that wouldn't ask for anything in return, I wasn't sure I was capable of it.

"We'll think about it," I replied.

Holden nodded, keeping his face devoid of emotion before he leapt into the air and was on all fours in the next instant. His light-grey wolf glanced back, piercing green eyes appraising every inch of me before he lifted his head and howled, likely signaling to his pack that he was headed home, as any good alpha should do.

I turned back to the city I hated and prayed to our creator

that this mate of mine would come soon. I wasn't sure how much longer I could stay.

The draw of the pack life was tempting. My wolf's needs grew with every day we failed to find our mate. All while the protective walls I'd built long ago vibrated with unease.

I hoped that finding our mate would bring a clarity I hadn't been able to grasp since watching my family be slaughtered.

4

ANDIE

The tea kettle screeched, making me jump from where I leaned against my counter. I turned to pull the pot from the stove and poured the steaming water into two waiting mugs.

Charlie was sitting impatiently at my table. She wanted to leave right away, but I was in no hurry to leave my home with a stranger. Not until I had some answer that made me feel more comfortable.

"We don't really have time for tea, Andie. As soon as Beatrix gets my message and tells me where to bring you, we have to leave," she said, but before I could respond, she read the cup I handed her and snorted. "'I didn't fall. I attacked the floor.' Why in the world do you have a coffee cup that says that?"

I shrugged, ignoring her mention of being in a hurry, and took a seat across from her. "My mom thought it was funny." And so did I.

Being a klutz was something to embrace instead of being

embarrassed about. I often found the more I tried to fight my penchant for hurting myself, the more accidents happened.

"I'm sorry about Aspen. When we knew she passed, our entire coven gathered to honor your mother. She might have chosen to leave, but she was still one of us." Charlie paused, meeting my stare. "As are you."

Everything about the woman in front of me was familiar, but I had no memory of her. I wanted to believe what she was saying, but I wasn't sure how to accept that the stories I'd heard as a child were true and that my mother had kept me from all of that.

I'd had a terrific relationship with my mother. We'd been more like sisters when I'd become a teenager. There wasn't a day that passed where I didn't miss her and the companionship that she'd offered me. She'd been the only constant in my life, the only person who hadn't judged me, used me, or left me. At least until she hadn't had a choice in the matter. Until one person's error had taken her life in a car accident.

"How do you know me?" I asked while swirling the English breakfast tea bag around my cup and doing my best not to let the anguish drown me.

Charlie took a sip of her tea and glanced at her phone before she answered me. "We were born on the same day, our moms were best friends, and until yours had to leave, so were we."

"I don't understand why you remember me, but I can't remember anything from before I was five."

It had always been that way for me. My mother had had pictures of me with my father before he'd died, but I didn't remember him, either. She'd said it was part of the grief and my mind's way of protecting me. Up until this moment, I'd never had a reason to believe otherwise.

Charlie checked her phone again and bit her bottom lip. "Um, I don't know if I'm allowed to say anything helpful. Honestly, I shouldn't have even been the one to find you. Dumb luck brought me here."

"What does that even mean?" I was trying to be patient, but I'd felt in the dark about a lot of things lately. Knowing someone was sitting right in front of me with plenty of answers, yet she was also unwilling to give them, wasn't helping my frayed nerves.

She sighed. "It means that Beatrix, our coven leader, was leading the search for you. There was a whole team assigned to find you, one I wasn't exactly part of. Instead of asking for their permission, I came to you as soon as I overheard someone in a club talking about a lost witch being located."

"Why would you assume that witch was me? *Am* I even a witch?" My stomach roiled at asking that last question. Denial had been my friend over the last several months while something inside me had been changing. While I'd recently begun to believe it was possible, I'd yet to truly accept that whatever was happening to me could be something that was supposed to be fictional.

"I don't know why I thought you were the witch they were talking about, but my gut told me I needed to know for sure either way. I listened long enough to get the name of this town, then followed the magic. Those two people were going to take you to another coven that has been trying to best us for centuries. They might have succeeded if you'd been taken."

I took another slow drink of my tea, trying to process

what Charlie was saying. I mean, I'd been there, had seen the whole thing, but now that there weren't crazy people after me and my adrenaline had calmed, hearing what had happened was hard to believe.

"I know this is a lot," Charlie said solemnly. "I thought you'd have known something about who you are, but then again, from what I've been told, your mother never wanted this life for you. Not after how your father died." She grimaced.

My face pinched. I really didn't want to ask the question, but after learning what little I had, there was a dreadful feeling in my gut that my father hadn't died of pancreatic cancer.

"How did he die?" I whispered and avoided her eye contact.

Charlie's hand reached across the table and covered mine. "There was an attack on our coven. He was trying to protect your mother and Junie, who was his only sister, in case you didn't know that."

Tears pricked at my eyes, my jaw tightened, and I wanted to scream. How could this be my life and I was only just finding out? None of it made sense, and I wished like hell my mother was here to fill in the many blanks.

"How could I not know any of this? Why did nobody tell me my father was one? How did my mother hide being a witch from me?" I asked, trying not to be hurt that she would have hidden this from me. That she left me to figure this all out on my own.

"I don't have all of the answers, but I wish I did if that helps. We really should be going, though. I know you're in pain, but if we don't go soon, things could get a lot worse," Charlie said, once again checking her phone.

My head shook. "Can you at least explain how my mom never showed any magic?" The thought that she betrayed me so severely had me frozen to my seat.

"From what I heard, Aspen asked to be stripped of her magic, which would explain why there were never any slip-ups for her to explain. She gave the energy to Juniper, who had no use for it, as she was already more powerful than she cared to be after your father died. Our coven was lucky to have her, and we were fortunate she was willing to share the magic with the coven, doing whatever it took to keep our members safe."

Juniper. My mother used to call Aunt Junie that when they'd been fighting. It used to make me giggle, especially when Aunt Junie would snicker behind Mom's back before apologizing for whatever had been done.

My chest tightened at the memories. I couldn't believe they were both gone. That there was no one else left in my family. That I was truly alone. Though, knowing my mom hadn't completely hidden everything from me, given she'd no longer had magic, did make me feel slightly better.

Charlie gave my hand another squeeze as a lone tear trailed down my cheek. Before I could ask anything else, her phone started to ring.

Charlie took a deep breath, then answered. "Hello, Beatrix."

"Where are you?" the woman's snippy voice bellowed from the speaker.

"In Montana," Charlie replied calmly.

"Why the hell are you still there? Did Moira's people get Andie?" Beatrix's voice darkened when she asked the second question, making me think she wasn't someone I wanted to piss off.

"No. Andie is right here next to me. I just wasn't sure where you wanted me to bring her."

"Well, I certainly didn't want you to keep her in the same place those idiots already found her in. Get to the coven. Now."

The call ended and Charlie let out another heavy sigh.

"Is everything okay?" I asked.

"Junie was Beatrix's best friend," Charlie explained. "Her passing has been hard on all of us, but mostly Beatrix. She'll be nicer to you, I promise. We really do need to go now that I know for sure where to bring you."

Her question made me recoil. "Where are we going? When will I be back? I have a job and rent to pay."

"I'm sorry, Andie. It's not safe for you to come back. More of those witches will keep coming until they get what they want." Her words and tone sounded sincere, but my anxiety was rising and all rationale had left me.

I pushed away from the table, taking several steps from Charlie and trying to push past the terror choking me. "How do I even know I can trust you? Where do you want to take me? I have to be able to come back. I have a job. People who depend on me. Rent to pay."

Charlie's fingers were flying over her phone when I finished my tirade of questions. Once she'd finished typing, her phone immediately dinged.

"You find there's something familiar about me, right?" Charlie asked, and I nodded. "Like I said before, you knew me prior to your memories being blocked. I can return them to you right now to help you trust me, but the spell can be painful. I'd rather not do that when we could be interrupted at any moment, but I can promise that as soon as we're settled at the coven, we'll give your past back to you. Once you remember, if you don't want to stay, we'll find somewhere safe for you, but here isn't that place. Not anymore."

The logical part of me knew Charlie was right. Those people had found me, and she hadn't killed the man. He could come back at any time, and I wasn't prepared to fight him off.

"What happened to the woman who was there?" I asked.

Charlie grimaced. "I killed her. She wouldn't relent like the man did. Killing isn't something we like to do, but you were in danger. It had to be done."

Magic and dead bodies. I wasn't mentally prepared to process whatever was going on here.

My legs began to ache, the sensation moving up through my stomach and across my chest. Then my hands warmed and began to glow a light pink—a rather new development that had my mouth falling open and a heaviness settling over my core.

"I'm sorry, Andie. We've run out of time. I tried to be patient, but what you're feeling right now? That's dark magic and that means more witches are close. We have to go. Now."

Charlie grabbed on to my wrist and the world fell out from under me just like before. I reached back and shoved her away from me as soon as we reappeared in a park. Or maybe it was a really big backyard. I didn't know and I didn't care.

I pointed at her with a snarl. "Don't you ever touch me again."

There was no stopping my freak-out. I'd been pushed to

my limits, and I needed a minute. Hell, I needed *days* to process not only what I'd learned, but also what I'd seen over the last hour. It didn't matter that I'd had assumptions about what was swirling inside me all these months. Up until now, my thoughts had been speculative. That had kept my sanity in check.

All of my assumptions were now reality, and I wasn't okay.

Charlie opened her mouth to reply, but I wasn't waiting around to hear what she had to say. My fury was on the rise, and I didn't want to say something to her that I didn't mean. In my heart, I was certain Charlie had meant well by ripping me from my home, but that didn't mean my mind was on the same page. Not yet.

My feet stomped heavily, carrying me forward and toward a fence. There was something shimmering around it, but I wasn't stopping. I had to find somewhere that I could be alone to process and figure out what I wanted to do.

I reached for the gate, and a calming sensation caressed my skin like an old friend, sending goosebumps along my arms and legs when I stepped through. A shudder rolled along my shoulders before I looked around.

To my left was a lone gravel road with no street signs or lights. On the right was more of the same road, but it wasn't empty. A massive dog stood frozen in place with ebony fur and glowing, blue eyes that were currently homed in on me.

I sucked in a breath, my legs beginning to shake uncontrollably. I rubbed my clammy palms over my eyes. Ignoring the rising hairs on the back of my neck, I lowered my hand and looked again, but the dog was gone.

"What the shit is happening to me?" I muttered.

"We're going to sort that out right now," a woman

whispered from behind me just before something pinched the skin between my shoulder blades.

I tried to turn around and see who was there, but my legs became jelly. As I felt the ground getting closer, a tiredness like I'd never known settled over me, and there wasn't a damn thing I could do about it.

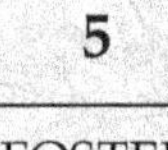

5

FOSTER

After Holden had left, I'd stayed on the ridge for another hour before the lure to head into the forest had called to not only my wolf, but myself as well.

It's her. She's here, he said excitedly.

Yeah, he'd thought that several times before when we'd caught what only turned out to be a lingering essence of the scent we'd been given. Each time it happened was more disappointing than the last. So, I wasn't holding my breath that this chase would be any different.

The transformation from man to animal came over me seamlessly when I pictured my wolf's ebony coat, sapphire eyes, and oversized paws. Warmth filled my chest and expanded throughout the rest of my body as it surged forward.

My wolf howled into the moon before racing toward the trees. *I feel her.*

There was a ball of heat growing inside my chest, making

me believe maybe my wolf was right this time. Maybe this mate of ours had finally arrived.

Hope was a bitch, though. More often than not, the emotion only let me down. So, I dashed the feeling away and focused on where my wolf was headed. He dodged around trees, paws practically flying over the forest's dirt floor. He was sprinting his way east, farther away from the city.

Do you know where you're going? I asked.

He was slow to respond, considering his answer carefully. *I think so. There is something there, muddling with the beacon I've been following.*

Something like magic?

My wolf's steps faltered, then his pace was suddenly faster than before. *I know where she is.*

Care to share? I asked.

Beatrix has her. At the coven.

We'd found the coven when we'd first arrived, but we'd stayed in the shadows, never making it known that we'd found their homes, a feat that should have been impossible knowing how strong Beatrix was, but she'd given no inclination that she was aware we knew where her coven resided.

I should have known then that there was a good chance our mate was a witch, but I hadn't been ready to admit anything to myself. It wasn't until we found the witch's house in the city that I truly allowed myself to think that way. As we got closer and closer to the magically charged stronghold, my heart confirmed what my thoughts had already assumed.

Our mate was a witch, and we were going to find her today.

Breathing became harder as we got closer to the coven and our heart raced twice as fast as we ran. We were so close, yet I wasn't sure how we were going to get within the witches' boundaries. Beatrix had a nasty shield over the property, and we hadn't been welcomed inside. At least, not yet.

We'll pace outside for as long as it takes for someone to let us in. My wolf snarled at the thought of being kept away from our mate.

Normally, I wasn't the rational one, but I could already tell that might change once we arrived.

I'll be fine. I know how to handle us *better than you*, he quipped.

He'd like to think so.

We arrived at the coven, slowing our pace to a trot and stepping onto the gravel street. Beyond the road, we could only see more trees, but I knew better.

Beatrix had an entire coven of witches hiding behind the shield I could sense but not see. The barrier put off vibes, warning us away, but that wasn't going to work anymore.

Regardless of any potential consequences, we would do whatever it took to see our mate and make sure she was safe. Whoever she was.

Do you think she knows we're here? my wolf asked.

I don't know. Witches don't share stories of their bonded pairs publicly, so I don't know how the connection works for them. Plus, we shouldn't have been able to tell where our mate was by a scent. At least not before we're bonded. With the Moon Goddess interfering, I doubt anything about what's to come will be what we expect.

We never physically saw our creator, but months ago, her essence appeared in our mind without warning. When she'd scared the hell out of us, I'd caught the slightest hint of amusement in her voice. I didn't particularly care for it, especially when she'd been so lean on details.

All she'd give us was a scent, dangling it in front of us like bait we couldn't deny. Roses and sage intertwined so uniquely that there would be no mistaking exactly who our mate was once she was close enough.

The Moon Goddess had gone just as quickly as she'd arrived. I'd tried to deny it had truly been her, but my wolf was relentless. He'd known the truth and forced me to see it as well.

You'll thank me soon enough, he said cockily.

Yeah, maybe.

My wolf stilled and the shield shimmered. We held our breath. It could be any witch, ready to cast us away, but something told me that wasn't going to be the case.

First, a jean-clad leg stepped through, followed by the rest of her body. I didn't get a chance to take in any details before I was ready to fall at the female's feet, promising her whatever she desired.

This was our mate. The one we'd been born to love and protect.

Except something wasn't right.

She wasn't searching for us like we'd been for her. She looked lost and confused and was furious about something as she scanned the area in front of her.

We took another step forward until she spotted us, and we froze again.

Fear quickly replaced every other emotion inside her.

She's scared of us. She doesn't know, my wolf whimpered.

I knew he was right, but this wasn't a bad thing. At least, not yet.

Her hands rubbed over her eyes, and I took that second to absorb as many details as I could about the woman I already knew I would die for.

Her long, thick hair was a pale pink that matched the rosiness of her cheeks. Plump lips sat below ocean-blue eyes I was instantly lost within. Her skin was like porcelain—creamy and without flaw.

My wolf lurched forward, bringing me out of my stupor just before she pulled her hands away from her face.

The bond was already forming for me. A steady thrum of *need* pulsed inside, but my instincts were telling me that we needed to have patience if we were going to do this right. Our mate wasn't ready for us, and we wouldn't push her to the point that we could lose her before we even had the chance to claim her. Not yet, anyway.

I forced my wolf back into the shadows and was going to wait to see what she did next, but then Beatrix appeared out of nowhere. The witch had a pinched expression, making the wrinkles on her old face stand out. She was dressed casually in matching charcoal linen pants and loose shirt. Something about her seemed frailer than I was used to seeing, but any sympathy I was beginning to have for the witch disappeared the moment she zapped my mate with magic.

In the next moment, I could taste my mate's panic, as could my wolf. He snarled and lunged forward. I should have stopped him, but I was just as furious that Beatrix would hurt our mate.

She tsked at us. "I don't think so, Wolf. I get her first."

Beatrix disappeared with our mate before my wolf could sink his teeth into her. Logically, I knew that was a good thing, but it was hard to be reasonable after what we just saw.

Why would she do that? My wolf snarled, failing to keep his temper in check, something that didn't happen often. He was usually the calmer one of us, but this time, I had a feeling he was going to need me.

I took a minute to consider what just happened. Our mate was scared and panicked and not okay. I'd like to believe that our presence would have eased some of her worries, but maybe we would have only made things worse.

I don't know, but we're not leaving until we do. Beatrix can't keep our mate hidden forever.

Are you sure about that? My wolf pressed.

I'll tear her precious coven apart if she attempts to, and the witch knows that.

I'd warned Beatrix several times that I'd do whatever it took to find my mate and keep her safe. I hadn't known then what she might need to be saved from, but the world was an ugly place. I'd seen that up close and personal on more than one occasion.

Beatrix could have the time she needed, but soon, we'd meet our mate. We'd make sure she knew exactly who we were to her, and that I was there to do whatever it took to make her happy and keep her safe.

6

ANDIE

I groaned when awareness slowly came back to me. My eyes didn't want to open, but I could feel uneven cushions under me, making me think I'd passed out in the living room instead of going back to my room the night before. I didn't remember drinking, but I sure as hell had a hangover.

My legs stretched over the arm of the couch, and the smooth material beneath my back confused me. Cautiously, I cracked one eye open, then winced when a bright light blinded me. This was not going to be a good day. Not with the headache that was already building between my eyes and the nightmares I was recalling from my dreadful night's sleep.

Witches. Massive dogs. Teleportation. Clearly, my imagination had officially gone off the rails.

I covered my eyes and sat up to take a few calming breaths. Keeping my eyelids down, I lowered my hands to the couch, noticing that there was leather instead of microfiber under me, but my brain was too muddled to properly question anything.

My body was sore in places it hadn't been for a long time. I braced myself before twisting my aching neck and sighing when it cracked several times on each side. Damn, that felt good.

With one more deep breath, I opened my eyes again and had to grip the cushions when my vision blurred. Queasiness erupted in my stomach, but the urge to get up and move was still strong. I didn't know why, but there was something I was supposed to be doing.

I fought against the nausea, forcing my eyes to stay open until the room finally came into focus, but I didn't bother standing when I saw what was in front of me.

"Not a nightmare," I muttered under my breath, wanting to cry in frustration at the realization that my world had indeed been flipped upside down.

Charlie was pacing behind the couch opposite me while an older woman sat there staring at me with a smirk on her face.

"Hello, Andie."

"I can't believe last night was real." My hands covered my face again and I leaned forward to rest my elbows on my scuffed-up knees.

No wonder I'd felt like I was hungover. I'd busted my hip and knees and had even fallen on my ass, all before fighting some crazy dude with magic and somehow surviving.

"It's still the same night. You've only been out about twenty minutes," the woman with long, grey hair and wrinkles around emerald eyes said. She was wearing a linen outfit that was dark grey in color and loose, almost grandmotherly, but her familiar annoyed tone told me she was anything but a sweet old lady.

I met the steady gaze of who I was pretty sure was Beatrix. "Where am I?"

The house was small, but there were minimal walls allowing me to see a modest kitchen, a three-person circle dining table, and a short hallway with two doors from where I sat on the couch.

"I'm Beatrix Jacobs, and you're in my home, which is inside the walls of the safest place for you. I'm aware that you didn't want to come here, but going back to your house would only be temporary. Those witches and warlocks will only continue to come for you now that they've located you once."

Her voice held no emotion, and I wasn't feeling welcomed. Charlie had been in a rush and yanked me into oblivion without my permission, but at least she'd been nice and understanding about all this craziness.

"Why should I believe anything you're saying? For all I know, you two could be the people I should be running from," I said even though I didn't mean the words. I was more so hoping for an explanation to questions I wasn't sure to ask.

"Your aunt was my best friend and, before you and your mother left, so was your mother. Those three seats over there were for us. A lot of spells and memories were created at that table. Now, I'm trying to honor both of their memories and keep you safe, given neither of them can do so any longer. You trying to run away isn't making this job very easy."

I opened my mouth to turn the tables and state things from my perspective, but before words could leave my mouth, Beatrix's hand lifted and wisps of something unreal escaped her fingers, aiming right for my chest.

When the silver energy penetrated my sensitive skin, I was forced to lean back into the cushions of the couch and was unable to move from the uncomfortable angle. Heat unfurled in my chest and spread toward my head, making my nausea worse.

"You need to remember, Andie. *We're* not going to hurt you," Beatrix said. "Well, this might cause you some discomfort, but you'll see a bit of pain is nothing compared to what you'll gain."

My teeth locked together, and my hands curled into fists, nails cutting into my palms. I tried to push through the needles poking at my mind and heart. Flashes of light flickered brightly around me, forcing my eyelids closed again.

Images came too fast for me to make sense of them, and feelings I didn't recognize or understand built inside me. A different kind of sorrow than I'd known before. An ache for things lost—people taken from me.

The throbbing lessened, and memories I'd never recalled before began to roll through my mind like an old slideshow. The first was me as a toddler with my father. He had the same auburn hair as I did as a child, with matching azure eyes. We were giggling and full of life, something I'd never known with him.

In my heart, I'd always loved the man in the pictures, but the nostalgic emotion I'd felt before was nothing like what this little girl portrayed. To her big saucer eyes, this man hung the moon and the stars.

Next was me, at maybe four years old, with a blonde girl my same age that reminded me a lot of the grown Charlie I knew was watching me now. We were covered head-to-toe in mud with matching grins and holding hands. She was the sister I'd never had. My person.

After that was my mother with her fair skin so much like mine, and Aunt Junie with her smile that everyone said I inherited. A younger version of Beatrix, this one with ebony hair instead of grey, is laughing with them in front of an older, modest house that I didn't think I'd ever seen before, but I immediately knew it had been my home. One filled with light and love and true happiness.

More snippets of me with the same people, but in different scenarios, kept appearing in my mind, all while tears trailed down my cheeks and I openly sobbed on the couch.

I rubbed my hand over the ache in my chest, trying to ease the burn that continued to grow there. I'd had a family and so much love, I should have exploded from it. From the perspective of a small child, everything in my life had been perfect. There wasn't anything I'd lacked or disliked before all of the joy had been ripped away from me.

As I wondered why I'd been taken from my home, the bright images in my head darkened. Suddenly, I was locked in a basement of some sort. There were shouts and loud sounds all around me and the smell of smoke, but I wasn't alone. The blonde girl I previously assumed to be Charlie was sitting next to me, squeezing my hand.

The latch above us creaked and our mothers' tear-stricken faces came into view. As soon as mine saw me, she wailed loudly and crumpled to the floor. Aunt Junie had to help us out while Charlie's mom consoled my mother. I couldn't see my father. I began screaming for my daddy, begging him to help Momma, but he never came.

And then? There was nothing.

The world I'd known had been torn from my memory. Stolen from a child who hadn't been old enough to understand, but one who'd been aware enough to know that nothing would ever be the same again.

The adolescent part of me didn't want to believe any of this was true, that my mother wouldn't have taken away everything good in our lives when we needed them most. Yet, as I reopened my eyes, there wasn't a doubt in my heart that I had known these people, cherished them even as a young child.

They had once been part of my everything, and I could depend on them.

It shouldn't have been that easy, but I believed my heart. I trusted the sense of familiarity I'd had instantly when I'd seen Charlie earlier. I trusted her words after she'd saved me. This was an anchor I could hold on to while I asked the hard questions. The ones I hoped didn't cast a shadow over the life I'd had with my mother.

With fresh tears still brimming in my eyes, I met Beatrix's stare, then Charlie's. "Why did we leave?"

Beatrix leaned forward, eyes softening toward me. "Your father died when our coven was attacked. Your mother was inconsolable. He was her soulmate, and losing him broke something inside her that could never be fixed. Within days of the battle, she begged me and Junie to take the magic from both of you, along with your memories. You were all she had left and, in your mother's eyes, taking you away from the life that stole half of hers was the only way to keep you safe. Aspen never meant to hurt you. She did the best she could for you and herself."

There was a small part of me that wanted to be furious

with my mother for taking this life from me, but somewhere deep inside me, her pain was also mine. Being older and having experienced losing her, then choosing to run away myself, I knew it wouldn't be right to fault her for the choices she'd made all those years ago.

Though, that rationale was hard to ignore when I saw Charlie with fresh tears in her own eyes, a friend who had been there for me, for as long as she could be, since the day we'd been born. She was the type of friend that I'd prayed for most of my life.

My mother had made a rash decision when she'd been filled with sorrow. One I wasn't sure had been the right one, given what I'd just seen, but I'd only been five. The memories I'd been given back were all sunshine and roses, but as an adult now, I knew not everything was as it seemed from the outside looking in.

Maybe my mother had known things I didn't. There had to have been something else besides losing my father that had set us on the path we'd taken, but even if I discovered what that could have been, I wasn't sure what I was supposed to do with the information.

"If Aunt Junie took my magic, why do my hands freak out and why are these other people after me?" I asked first, since it was more relevant than dwelling on the past I couldn't change.

Charlie finally came and sat down next to me, grabbing my hand. "Junie wouldn't take your magic at first. She didn't agree with your mother's choice, but she wanted to support Aspen the best she could. So, instead of taking your magic, Junie masked it. Only, you were stronger than she'd suspected, and your mother found out."

"Is that why my aunt stopped coming around?" She'd

been at my ninth birthday, then I'd never seen her again. My mom had said Junie had gone off on her own adventure and had always given different, short answers about what that meant until I'd finally stopped asking.

Beatrix nodded. "Junie was heartbroken that day. She'd tried to slowly prepare you for who you'd be one day, but you zapped your mother by accident when she told you that you couldn't stay the night with your aunt. I'm not sure what happened in the end, only that your mother made Junie do something more permanent with your magic, then asked her to never come back. Clearly, that something wasn't removing it entirely."

"If my mother didn't have magic, then why did Aunt Junie listen?" In my mind, I was really asking: *Why hadn't my aunt fought to see me if she'd known the truth? Why hadn't she come for me when my mother had died? Why had I been left so alone and broken?*

"Your mother threatened to give your magic to another coven. The same one that's after you now. It was a twisted, but effective threat. After your mother passed, Junie tried to find you, but by the time we found out, you'd already disappeared. The spell that Junie cast when you were young had done such a good job of concealing you that even she couldn't track you when she needed to most," Beatrix answered.

My chin trembled and my stomach fell out from under me. I'd been so close to having all this back, but I'd run. Three years wasted being sad and alone and not feeling good enough. Maybe it was better if I didn't get these answers. Maybe ignorance truly was bliss.

Even as I thought the words, I knew that wasn't true. I

just had to find the strength to keep my head up and keep talking.

"If Aunt Junie cast the spell, couldn't she have tracked her own magic instead of tracking me?" I asked, assuming locating spells were as easy as fiction made them seem.

Charlie answered with ire lacing her words. "No, because you helped her cast the spell. A condition from your mother to make sure Junie couldn't interfere again."

Never had the urge to speak to my mother been so strong. I didn't want to be angry with her, but learning all of this made it harder by the second. I needed to understand why she'd tried so hard to keep me isolated.

"When Junie died during a supernatural battle, any existing spells she'd had active in the world ceased to exist," Beatrix explained. "Because your power was intertwined with the concealment spell, it helped you stay hidden for far longer than any of us liked. Now that the spell is slowly breaking, you have a choice to make, Andie." Beatrix's voice hardened, losing the softness she'd momentarily been showing.

I straightened my shoulders and lifted my chin. "What choice would that be?"

"Do you want to be a witch? Or do you want to start a new life with no more magic left inside you, no danger of attracting a coven's interest, like your mother wanted?"

Charlie's fingers flinched around my hand. I didn't know who she was anymore, but now I remembered the girl with who I'd been best friends. The one who'd climbed trees with me, so we could practice magic without our parents finding us. The one who'd hugged me tightly enough to keep the pieces of my heart together when my hamster had died. The one who had always known how to make me laugh.

I'd been alone for a long time. The weirdness I'd been fighting against over the last several months was frightening, but did I want to live the rest of my life wondering *what if*? Even if that was what my mother had thought was best?

My first instinct was to stay and face whatever was happening. This was my home, and these people had once been my family, but I still had my mother's wishes to consider. There was a reason she'd walked away. Would I be tarnishing what we'd had by coming back to this life after all these years?

"Does Andie have to decide now?" Charlie asked, breaking the tense silence.

Beatrix narrowed her eyes on my friend before turning back to me. "I suppose not, but there is something else you need to know. Something that might be helpful with your decision."

I wanted to revert back to my childish ways and roll my eyes at the old witch but managed to refrain from the action. Of *course* there was something else, given she'd likely read my hesitancy. Why wouldn't there be?

"What's that?" I asked begrudgingly.

"Are you aware that witches have soulmates?" Beatrix asked.

"Outside of the fact that you used that word earlier to describe my parents, not really. Unless you count what I've seen in the movies. Please, don't tell me I have to find one to be welcomed back here."

Beatrix recoiled from my last sentence. "Gods, no. Being tied to someone is not a requirement we have here. But yes, your parents were soulmates, something that is rather rare for our kind. So rare that we don't talk about them much, but I believe you have one."

I searched the old witch's face, hoping to find some hint that she was lying and trying to dangle some happily-ever-after in front of me in hopes that it would sway my decision in a positive way. Except she gave nothing away other than candor.

"How do you know?" I asked, my hands beginning to shake from the overload of emotions.

Charlie gasped. "That wo—"

Beatrix cut her off with a wave of the hand. "There's a man who's been around and he's waiting outside, but you don't have to meet him if you don't want to. You're not going to be forced into this life if it's not one that you want. There are risks, as you now remember, but they're just as great outside the barriers of this coven."

For the first time since I'd sat up on the couch, Beatrix made me feel as though she truly wanted me to stay and learn about the life I'd been taken from. I hadn't taken her for the mushy type, so I wasn't expecting anything grand from the witch, but she wasn't pushing me out the door, either.

That, combined with the memories I was still trying to process, told me what I was already going to decide. Except, knowing there was a soulmate waiting for me just outside? I wasn't sure what I was supposed to do with that information.

There was a warmth in my chest expanding that wasn't like what I was used to. It wasn't like I'd never had boyfriends before, but there had never been any serious relationships. I mostly considered them casual flings I only had to keep the worst of my loneliness away.

"Does he live here? In your coven?" I asked Beatrix, because that definitely made a difference.

She and Charlie shared a look I didn't like. Almost as if they were silently arguing in their heads and Charlie had won, or at least refused to back down because she answered me instead.

"Your soulmate doesn't live in the coven. He isn't even a warlock. Do you remember anything about the other supernatural races?" she asked, and when I couldn't find the words to answer, she continued. "Let's keep it simple for now since you've already been overwhelmed enough today."

"That would be appreciated," I croaked.

Charlie continued, "Your soulmate is a wolf shifter. He's been searching this area for you for months and none of us knew it was you until tonight. I don't know anything about him, but I do know that wolf mates are the most common. Knowledge of them is rather public, unlike with our kind. They're loyal to a fault and I don't believe you have anything to fear from him, but I have no problem putting the fear of God in him to be sure."

My breathing became erratic, and I leaned forward to put my head between my knees. Maybe I shouldn't have asked. Maybe I should have taken more time to process one thing at a time. Learning that I had a soulmate was one thing but finding out he was a mother-freaking wolf was something else entirely.

"You're welcome to turn him away. I would support that decision," Beatrix said.

Her words had me looking up and curious as to why she would say that. She'd previously made soulmates sound like something to be revered. Now she was suggesting it was okay to turn mine away? I had a feeling she possibly didn't approve of this man or wolf or whatever I was supposed to call him.

"Is there something wrong with him?" I asked.

"Outside of the fact that he's a wolf? Not necessarily," Beatrix replied with an air of disgust.

Something about how much the old witch didn't like this man made me want to meet him, regardless of how freaked out I was.

"If I choose to meet him, does that mean…anything?" I asked.

Charlie shook her head. "No. We're not sure if your connection with him will be like the ones shared between witches or wolves, but either way, there is a process. One that doesn't immediately tie you to him."

The ache in my chest was loosening and less about the situation I'd been thrown into was seeming all that crazy. I wasn't sure if that was because of the memories I was given back, I'd reached a level of freak-out that made me numb, or something else entirely, but in that moment, I decided I was done running.

I loved my mother, and I didn't blame her for the choices she'd made, but I wanted something more out of my life than spending the rest of it alone and scared of what I now knew.

With a conviction I didn't think I was capable of, I said, "I want to meet him."

7

FOSTER

Nearly an hour had passed since Beatrix had disappeared back into her compound with my mate. I didn't even know the female's name, but her soft eyes and creamy skin were permanently burned into my memory.

We'd stayed in the road, waiting for her to come back to us, to need us the same way we'd been needing her all these months, but the longer our mate was behind the witches' barrier, the farther away she felt from us.

We need to get her, my wolf said evenly.

She was scared of us.

What I should have said was she'd feared the big wolf leering at her, but my wolf didn't need that.

She just doesn't understand. Once she does, she won't be afraid anymore, he pleaded.

My wolf's hurt was plaguing me, increasing my own. I hadn't wanted a mate, but all it had taken was one look into her innocent blue eyes for everything to change for me. Suddenly, I longed to hold the one meant just for us.

Knowing that she was just out of reach...that was more painful than having spent months searching for her aimlessly.

The shield next to us shimmered and another witch stepped out, one I wasn't familiar with. She was older like Beatrix, but instead of grey hair, this one had stark, white strands with hazel eyes.

"Shift, Wolf," the woman demanded.

My wolf snarled at her. *She doesn't get to tell us what to do.*

Agreed, but if we want to see our mate sooner rather than later, we're going to have to play nice.

The roles between my wolf and I were reversed, and I wasn't sure how I felt about that. Regardless, I didn't have time to argue with him. I pushed the shift forward, picturing my human form and the clothes I'd been wearing before.

Within seconds, I was back on two feet and looming over the witch. "Where's my mate?"

"She's inside and safe. Beatrix said you can come in on two conditions." She spoke with an attitude that told me this witch wasn't in agreement with her leader.

"What are they?" I asked.

"You're not allowed to shift to your wolf form while on coven lands, and if Andie wants you to go, then you'll leave without argument."

Andie. Our mate's name was Andie.

Andie, my wolf echoed.

The tomboy name wasn't what I'd expected from the female we'd seen, but the more I repeated the word, the more it suited her.

"You have my word that we won't shift, and I will do whatever it is that my mate needs, even if that means walking away from her," I said to the witch, even though just saying the words caused my chest to constrict. I wasn't sure what I'd do if Andie found us unworthy.

She won't turn us away. It's not possible, my wolf said, finding some of his positivity again.

I wanted to believe he was right, but finding Andie this way wasn't how things usually worked. The Moon Goddess would never have involved herself under normal circumstances. I wasn't counting on anything about this arrangement being the way we expected.

The old witch huffed, then turned her back on me. She pressed her hand against the shield, and a silver glow emitted between the barrier and her palm. When she pulled away, the shape of a door formed.

"Go through before it closes. I won't open it again," the witch snapped.

As much as I wanted to bite her head off—literally—I needed to get inside the coven, and this was the only way. I'd hold my tongue long enough to get to Andie, then re-evaluate how *nice* I needed to be to these witches if they wanted to continue having an attitude toward me.

The witch stomped deeper into the coven, and I followed her, ignoring everything around me when the presence of our mate ignited inside me. My chest swelled, and I was breathless for the first time in my life, letting my feet carry me forward.

We arrived at a courtyard and the witch pointed to a bench. "Sit."

"No," I snarled back.

She raised a brow at my actions.

"Just because I'm not your guest doesn't mean you get to treat me with disrespect," I added with a more even tone.

"Noted," was all the old biddy said before disappearing into the shadows.

I was left alone in a stone courtyard filled with empty benches, a three-tier water fountain in the middle, some statues of women and men standing with their hands held out in front of them, and a few canvas awnings strung just a few feet above my head.

The crescent moon was peeking through the space between the coverings and warming my skin. I inhaled deeply and closed my eyes. The Moon Goddess had sent us on one hell of a goose chase. I didn't want to have hope that all the running and searching we'd done was finally at an end, but the wisps of excitement were hard to ignore.

That was until my shadowed soul stepped in and reminded me that by finding this mate of ours, by letting her in and caring about her, she was just another person for us to lose. Another light to be smothered by our darkness.

Regardless of that, I wasn't willing to turn away from Andie. She needed me. I didn't know why, but I knew my creator wouldn't have interfered as she had if that wasn't the case. I was going to find out and do whatever it took to keep her safe.

The click of heels connecting with the concrete walkway echoed from behind me. I tensed and turned slowly, expecting to see Andie, only to be disappointed by the sight of another witch.

A blonde female, maybe in her early twenties, was headed for me. She wore a smirk on her full lips, but there was concern etched into her cognac eyes.

She flicked her golden hair back. "Foster, I presume?"

"Who are you?" I demanded.

"I'm someone you're going to want to be nice to if you're who Beatrix has told me you are."

A growl built in my chest. "There is no one other than Andie that I *need* to be nice to."

She let out a small laugh. "I'm Charlie. Andie was my best friend before she left our coven, and I will protect her with my life. Even from you. She's going to come out here, and you're going to stay calm. More specifically, your wolf isn't allowed to maul Andie the moment he sees her. She knows you're a shifter and her soulmate, but this is all new to Andie. She's going to need time to adjust. If you can't give her that, then you and I will be seeing each other again real soon."

I wanted to be furious that the young witch was speaking to me that way, but her words were nothing other than true. My wolf was rather good at sensing truth from lie, and nothing about her threats were false to him. I didn't want to share my mate, but given my history, it wasn't necessarily a bad thing to have more people around Andie who would fight to keep her safe.

"I won't do anything to hurt Andie. You have my word," I said to the young witch.

She nodded, then turned back, exiting the way she'd arrived.

I like Charlie, my wolf said.

Is that all? He'd been quieter than normal, and I needed to know if he'd sensed something I hadn't.

This meeting doesn't have anything to do with me. I'll have my moment with Andie when the time is right, he replied.

As eager as my wolf had been to find our mate, I wasn't sure how to take his current mood, but before I could further question him, more footfalls echoed from the shadows.

I bit the inside of my cheek and leaned forward, trying to see if another annoying witch was headed my way, or if I'd finally get to see my mate again.

As the pounding in my chest began reverberating in my ears, I knew it wasn't just any witch getting closer.

With bated breath, I took another step toward the shadows, and the glow of Andie's light-pink hair first appeared, followed by her light blue eyes, angelic skin, and rosy cheeks.

My hands itched to reach out to her, but I forced myself to stay where I stood.

Andie's steps slowed when our gazes met, and it took every strength I contained not to fall at her feet. There was an eruption of possessiveness inside me that I hadn't expected, but as I fought the need to wrap my arms around her, I also knew I wasn't the only one affected.

A flush crept up Andie's neck, coloring her oval face while she appraised me with heated eyes. Her mouth parted and I watched her tongue slowly peek out, wetting her lips. She leaned closer to me, tilting her head slightly to the right.

I thought she was going to say something, but instead, the glow of pink emanating from her hands distracted us both.

Without thinking, I was standing inches from her and held both of her hands in my own. Any previous thoughts quickly dissipated when the heat from her magic moved up my forearms.

The energy wrapped around me, drawing us closer together. I knew I was supposed to give Andie space, but when I searched her face, there was only awe shining through her azure eyes.

Andie's magic faded away, and I expected her to

withdraw from my hold, but instead, she looked up at me, offering a small smile. "Hi."

"I'm Foster," I said awkwardly.

"Nice to meet you, Foster. I'm Andie."

"I know."

She sighed. "Seems to be the case with all of the people I'm meeting tonight."

I grimaced, realizing I'd struck a nerve with her already. "The other witch already told me your name. I don't know anything else about you, though."

Her smile reappeared. "Except that I'm supposed to be your soulmate, right?"

Apparently, this woman wasn't as fragile as she looked.

"So I've been led to believe," I replied.

"How do you know? Did someone tell you?" she asked, her brow furrowing slightly.

"Normally, we have to see our mates to know, but there was some intervention from my creator that made me drawn to this area. I've felt you right here for months now." I placed one of her hands over my chest. "I just didn't know who you were until tonight."

She bit her lip while shaking her head. Frustration rolled off her in waves with an undertone of surprise. "Creator? What does that mean? Do you not have normal parents? Sorry, not a lot of this makes sense to me yet, and none of it is what I expected."

I didn't want to further overwhelm her, so I moved to take a step back before answering her questions, but when I did, her fingers dug into my forearm, an action that seemed to be as unexpected by her as it was by me.

She stiffened, then loosened the hold she had on me. I

took several steps back. My right hand rubbed the back of my neck while the other made a fist at my side.

Does she not feel the bond? I demanded from my wolf, even though I knew he wouldn't have the answer.

There's something wrong with her magic.

What do you mean?

I can sense that something is missing from her. I don't know what, but there has to be a way to fix this and we're going to figure it out, he replied earnestly, but there was an underlying nervousness he was trying and failing to hide from me. Neither of us would survive her rejection if that happened.

"To answer your previous question, when I say creator, I don't mean the person who gave me life in the human sense. She's the one who gifted me the wolf inside me, who created all of the wolf spirits that shifters have inside them."

She nodded, fidgeting with her fingers. "Right. Wolves. I almost forgot about that part."

When Andie finished speaking, she was looking everywhere but at me. I don't know what I did or said to make her more nervous than she'd been just a moment ago, but I had to fix this.

If I didn't, that would be a darkness I was certain I wouldn't be able to come back from.

w.samaiya.com

8

ANDIE

For a moment, I had found my resolve, a strength I wasn't sure I had within me, but that feeling became muddled as soon as I'd seen Foster. He'd been standing there, a beast of a man, with this tortured look in his stormy blue eyes that calmed the moment our gazes had connected.

Instantly, I'd wanted to go to him. To heal whatever ailed him. My fingers itched to trail over the scruff on his cheeks, to get lost in the long strands of his nearly black hair, but the attraction I'd immediately felt for him had been dashed away by the appearance of my magic, something that until that night, nobody else had seen besides me.

Instinct had me wanting to hide, but before I could do so, Foster was in front of me. One touch from him had my energy exploding. When the magic wrapped itself around Foster, I thought that was the beginning of feeling the connection to him as a soulmate, but instead, things had only gotten confusing.

Fear, desire, shock, and so many other mixed emotions ignited within me, making it impossible to know what I was supposed to do. Even more so when Foster's disappointment practically smacked me in the face after I'd confessed to my confusion.

Maybe I didn't know what a bond felt like, but based on what Charlie had said, I'd expected to just *know* in my heart, and I didn't. There had definitely been a physical reaction— one to which my magic and libido had both clearly reacted— but the deeper emotional connection hadn't been there.

Even so, there wasn't an inch of him I hadn't taken in with my eyes, beginning with his wide shoulders, on to his black-and-grey tattoo-covered arms, his muscled thighs, and all the way down to his well-worn brown boots.

But his physical attributes hadn't been what called to me most. It had been the lost look in his eyes, the contrived tone with which he'd spoken when I'd hurt him with my words, the way my magic had wanted me to keep touching him.

Still, there was nothing deep in my heart, beyond my neglected sex drive, which yearned for him.

The fact that I was saddened by that thought was another reason for my shock, and I had no idea what I was going to do about it.

Worse was how quiet he had become. There was tension around us that continued to grow stronger, so I spoke again, trying to find the words to make this less awkward.

"What I meant before when I said this wasn't what I expected is that Beatrix and Charlie tried to prepare me for meeting you, and I'm not sure this is something anyone can prepare for. I'm not saying I don't believe there's a connection between us. I just don't want to pretend there's this magical moment for me in which I just know. I might not know you, but I'd like to think you deserve better than lies from me on our first meeting."

His eyes moved to mine again, and both of his hands loosened at his sides. "I appreciate you not lying." He stepped closer again. "My wolf thinks there is something… off with your magic."

"My magic? Why?" I asked with an elevated voice for two reasons. The first being that I didn't like hearing something else might be wrong. The second reason was that I still hadn't quite accepted the whole wolf soulmate thing.

It wasn't like I didn't know as a child that shifters existed, but I'd never officially met one. I knew very little about them, and I needed to focus on one problem at a time. My magic was of the most concern.

I wasn't just a human with something freaky happening to her. I was a witch who belonged to a coven with another coven after me and a man—correction—wolf shifter standing before me who was supposed to be my soulmate. Mind freaking blown.

Before Foster could answer me, a dizziness rocked through me, breathing became harder, and I had the urge to flee again. I squeezed my eyes shut and pressed my palms over my ears, swaying back and forth.

The sudden panic attack was just another thing I hadn't expected. I'd been handling things mostly well since Beatrix had given me my memories back. Too well, in fact. The clarity with which I was able to recall my time in this coven was unnatural, considering I'd only been five when we left.

But I couldn't deny as more memories surfaced that they were real and mine, appearing as high-quality movie reels instead of the fuzziness I would have expected from a child's mind. It was as if I'd been hyperaware from the moment I'd been born.

Any calm those memories had brought me was wearing off and I was no longer okay. Foster had said there was something wrong with my magic, and this freak-out was proving him right.

Foster wrapped his arms around me, and I froze for a split second before allowing his warmth to ease my worries. His hug seemed to be the remedy I hadn't known I needed.

He was a stranger to me, but there was something soothing about his touch. Not only had he calmed my magic, but he seemed to be doing the same for my heart while he held me.

"I didn't mean to upset you. Whatever my wolf senses, it probably has more to do with the bond than you," Foster said, taking responsibility for my meltdown, which I hadn't blamed him for.

I took a shuddering breath and rested my head against his chest. He was so much taller than I was, but every dip and curve between us fit perfectly together as his hands splayed over my back, holding me securely.

"What are you doing to her?" Charlie's voice sneered from behind us.

Foster's arms tightened around me. "None of your damn business."

I turned my head enough to see Charlie. She pointed a glowing finger at Foster. "I warned you, Wolf."

"Whoa. Everything is fine. I had a bit of a freak-out that was self-induced. Foster didn't do anything other than calm me down," I said while trying and failing to twist further around.

A rumble vibrated beneath my head from Foster's chest, making my stomach warm and my heartrate increase. My physical responses to him made me think that maybe there were signs of the bond there if I paid close enough attention and they just needed time to grow.

Charlie dropped her arm, her eyes roaming over me. "You're really okay?"

"I am."

Foster's hold was still secured around my waist, but I was finally able to turn around and face Charlie. She was still glaring at Foster, and I worried about them not getting along, which seemed ridiculous. I didn't know him, and I technically didn't know Charlie anymore.

Yet, there was something inside me that knew both of these people were important to whatever was coming next. Along with knowing that their places in my life weren't negotiable. It was a fact that should have freaked me out, but there was an underlying peace that settled over the thought, preventing any further unraveling of my emotions from happening. At least for the moment.

Charlie smirked. "Do you remember that one time when you got mad at me for eating the last brownie?"

Brownie? I had to think about that for several moments before the memory surfaced. I choked back a laugh. "I do, but I'm not sure why you'd bring it up now."

She nodded at Foster. "Just a reminder that you're stronger than you might think. You don't have to be anywhere that you don't want to be."

I assumed by *anywhere*, she meant in Foster's arms and not at the coven. "Noted," I said, then I felt Foster stiffen behind me.

"That's enough, Charlie." Beatrix's voice sounded before

she waltzed into the courtyard, then she nodded at Foster. "Release her. She's safe here and you know it."

"Then why was she trying to run away when I first saw her?" Foster growled in reply.

"First, be thankful I didn't turn you into a toad for trying to bite me earlier. I won't soon forget that particular transgression and I expect it not to happen again if you want to stay within my coven. Secondly, Andie didn't remember this was home when she first arrived, but she knows now. Don't you, Andie?" Beatrix asked.

I glanced back up at Foster. "You tried to bite her?"

"She made you go unconscious and took you away without explanation. Something she knew damn well would set my wolf off after only just seeing you for the first time."

"Okay." I probably should have asked more questions about that, but Beatrix was tapping her foot in my direction, seemingly still waiting on me to answer her questions.

I wanted to agree with Beatrix that this place was indeed my home, but I hesitated to give my answer freely. I didn't want to be so comfortable with these people and this place that I ended up following along blindly with whatever they said. Regardless of the familiar feelings, I had to make sure I was taken seriously.

"This coven was and could still be my home, but the more I remember, the more questions I have. I need to have a clear picture of everything before we make anything final," I finally replied.

Beatrix's lips thinned. "Well, let's go somewhere and chat, then." She headed down the pathway to our left, and Charlie followed after her. The fact they just expected me to follow was the exact reason I was attempting to be cautious, no matter how much I also wanted this to be home and have a piece of the family I remembered once having.

Foster loosened his hold on me when Charlie and Beatrix disappeared. "You're better now," he said as a statement instead of a question.

"I am. How do you seem so sure of that?" I asked.

Foster's shoulders softened, and he lightly gripped my elbows, sending shivers along my skin before he even opened his mouth.

"It's my purpose, Andie. To know how you're feeling, to keep you safe, to be whatever you need me to be. I understand you don't feel the same connection, but that doesn't lessen what I'm experiencing. I can't help who I am, but I will protect you even if you can't reciprocate my feelings."

There was an underlying pain in his words, an ache that was overdue for healing.

My heart and head were conflicted over what the man before us was supposed to be. I believed he felt a connection to me, but soulmate or "mate," as he'd said? That, I couldn't be certain of. At least not until I had more information.

Beatrix reappeared next to us. "Are you coming?" she asked me specifically.

"Yeah, I just needed a minute."

She turned to Foster. "I'm sure I'll see you soon."

Foster's eyes darkened, and he towered over the older witch. "I'm not letting her leave my sight until I know what's going on and that she's safe. You understand that even if you don't like it, so don't try to stop what's happening."

Beatrix began raising her hand, but I placed mine over

hers. "If things are as bad as you've hinted at, wouldn't it be helpful to have someone else around who wants to make sure I don't end up with the wrong witches?"

She grimaced. "I suppose."

"And you *did* let him into the coven. From what I'm remembering, only other race leaders were ever allowed within these walls and even then, it was rare." There had been an alpha wolf who'd arrived one day that had my mother and Charlie's gossiping like crazy in front of us. I hadn't known what it meant then, but I understood the importance now.

"Maybe I shouldn't have given you those memories back," Beatrix complained.

"Then you'd be *forcing* me to stay here, and I don't think that's what anyone wants," I replied, then I nodded at Foster, noticing his tense jaw and the glare in his eyes. "He stays for now. I don't know exactly what's going on, but I'm certain we all need to be on the same page before things get worse."

Foster's intense gaze lessened at my words.

I wasn't sure what the long-term solution was, but I needed to know why another coven was after me. More importantly, I needed to know how to make sure they didn't get their hands on me.

Foster placed his palm over my lower back. Beatrix huffed and turned around. We followed her down a stone pathway. There were little cottages, most with their lights on, but the shutters on all of them were closed.

Beatrix opened the door to a building at the end, and Charlie was standing near the entryway. She let out a breath and smiled at me when I appeared, showing off a small dimple on her left cheek.

The space was completely open with no other rooms inside. A fireplace was warming the large, open room, and there were three black couches along with several wooden chairs facing the dimly lit fire.

Cream walls surrounded us with abstract paintings placed throughout. My attention caught on one of them and I walked closer, taking in the burst of colors that melded together. Greens and blues on the left with reds and oranges on the right and an explosion of yellow in the middle tying them together.

"Your mother painted that as a representation of your family," Beatrix said from behind me.

My fingers traced over the textured canvas. "It's beautiful. Just like she was."

The ache in my chest, the one that had ripped open from the loss of my mother, grew. I wished more than anything that she was here with me now. That she'd been the one to prepare me for whatever was happening. Knowing that Aunt Junie was also gone…that was a sorrow I wasn't ready to face.

"Come sit," Beatrix said, and I turned for the couch.

Foster was still standing near the door, stiff in the shoulders, with dark eyes that scanned the room multiple times.

I considered telling him to come with me but stopped myself and took a seat in the middle of the nearest couch. Charlie joined me, a grin growing on her face.

"What are you smiling about?" I asked.

"I have wished for this day ever since you left. The fact that you're not running for the hills right now makes everything else seem like a cakewalk."

"I mean, I did run at first, but in my defense, you teleported me twice without my permission," I said lightly.

"You're alive. That's all that matters."

Charlie's words sobered me, reminding me that if she hadn't been there, I very likely could have died, or *wished* I had.

A shadow loomed over me, and the brush of Foster's fingers curling around the back of the couch caused tingles to run across my shoulders. It was as if he'd known my thoughts had taken a turn and couldn't stop himself from being there for me.

The thought had my mind racing and my chest warming, but something told me I wasn't going to figure out Foster until I understood what was happening with myself, so I began asking my questions.

"Who were those people after me? Charlie mentioned that they were going to use me to gain entry to a coven they shouldn't even want to belong to," I said to Beatrix once she sat in a chair closer to the fire.

"I don't know who they were specifically, but Charlie was right. A witch named Moira Grimm has made it known to those who like to dabble in dark magic that if they can bring you to her, then she will reward them."

I knew that name. More accurately, the last name. When all witches turned five, they began learning of our heritage and the importance of protecting our magic.

"She's from one of the original founding families," I said.

Beatrix grinned proudly. "I'm glad to see the memories I unlocked are coming to use already."

"Memories? Why did you need to unlock them?" Foster asked, still standing guard behind me.

Beatrix sighed, no longer smiling. "Because they were

taken away to make things easier. The story is too long to explain. Just try to keep up."

A rumble vibrated from Foster's chest, and I looked up to find him grinding his teeth and sneering at Beatrix. I didn't blame him for being pissed. She wasn't being welcoming to him, but I didn't feel right saying anything. Being in the middle of these two was less fun than getting attacked earlier, especially when I knew so little.

"As are you and I. Jacobs, Bishop, Proctor, Howe, and Grimm."

I didn't remember that, but as soon as Beatrix said my last name, I recalled the pride my father used to have in our family name and history. He would tell stories of our ancestors who fought for what was right and believed in taking care of the coven as a whole instead of only worrying about themselves.

That same pride he had rose within me, overshadowing the pressure I suddenly felt to live up to the family name.

Beatrix continued, "Only two covens contain direct lines to our founding families now. Proctor and Howe lines died out decades ago, leaving just ours and Moira's. She's not a fan of being outnumbered."

"So, what does that mean? She wants me to join her? Wouldn't it have been smarter to *ask* me instead of trying to kidnap me?"

Foster snarled from above me, clearly not handling all of this information well.

Beatrix ignored his outburst and answered, "She doesn't want you to join her. Moira wants to take your family magic and make herself the most powerful witch to ever exist."

"How can that happen?" I asked while trying not to be

concerned with the sound of splintering wood coming from the back of the couch, thanks to Foster.

Charlie grimaced next to me. "Unless it's given willingly, like your mother did when the two of you left, there's only one way. Moira would have to kill you herself."

9

ANDIE

Foster's hands moved from the back of the couch to my arms. His fingers curled around my biceps, and I thought for a moment that he was going to pick me up.

"This witch you speak of, where is she?" Foster demanded.

"Settle down, Wolf," Beatrix said. "You can't just show up at her coven and kill her yourself. She might have a small following, but they practice in dark magic. That makes them unpredictable. We suspected this day would come, and we have contingencies."

The heat pouring from Foster settled on my neck, and he leaned over me, keeping gentle pressure on my arms. "Explain."

His one word packed a wave of power I didn't understand. The energy in the room cackled while Beatrix glared at Foster.

"You can't show up here demanding information from

me when you've been keeping *that* little trick a secret. What else are you hiding, *Alpha* Wolf?" Beatrix asked.

Charlie gasped and turned to look up at Foster while I had no clue what the big deal was. I was slowly remembering that wolves, vampires, and even fae were real, but I didn't know the details of each race. The teachings I'd only begun to learn before leaving the coven hadn't extended beyond witches.

I wasn't sure why it was such a big deal that Foster was an alpha. I mean, I knew they were leaders of their packs, but wouldn't that be a good thing? Or was I supposed to be freaking out some more and completely missing the cue?

"Nothing that concerns you, Witch. I'm here for one reason only, and that's to keep Andie safe. So, whatever it is you know about Moira and any contingencies you have, I have the right to know about them."

I stood, wanting to put a stop to the arguing and figure out why these two were constantly at each other's throats, but before I could get any words out, I ended up right back on my ass. Electricity sizzled over my chest, and the room broke out into chaos.

Foster leapt over the couch, including me and Charlie, then he pinned Beatrix to the wall. Two other witches, one older with white hair and the other younger with short ebony hair, stormed through the front door and flung streams of magic at Foster's back, but he didn't budge from his position over Beatrix.

"You hurt her," he snarled, and spittle from Foster landed on the older witch.

Beatrix's eyes widened momentarily before she glared at him. "I was aiming for you."

"And you expect me to entrust my mate with this

coven?" Foster spat, giving her another hard shove into the wall. I swore I saw signs of claws where his fingers should have been.

Charlie moved into my line of sight, pressing her hand over my chest and taking away the stabbing sensation that was making it hard for me to breathe.

"Are you okay?" she asked, her eyes roaming over me.

I brushed my hands over myself to be sure. "Yeah, I felt more paralyzed than anything else. Thanks for whatever you just did."

"Of course."

Charlie helped me up and began to guide me toward the other two witches, who were inching closer with their hands out, ready to act again when needed, but standing down for the moment.

I pulled out of Charlie's hold, wanting to prevent things from escalating further.

"I wouldn't get in the middle of that," Charlie warned.

"I kind of already did," I replied, rubbing the sore spot over my heart where Beatrix had zapped me.

I hadn't even seen the magic coming. Beatrix was more powerful than I remembered, and I worried Foster was going to bite off more than he could chew when it came to her. Maybe even literally.

Even though he'd let go of Beatrix while I'd been distracted, he hadn't stepped very far away from her. They were berating each other in hushed tones when I approached, and they stopped when they saw me.

Foster moved closer to me, and his dark eyes trailed over my chest and arms, inspecting every inch before he met my stare. I ignored the warmth that unfurled in my stomach and nodded at him. "I'm okay."

"You might not have been," he grumbled.

"I know, and I think Beatrix has learned her lesson." I gave her a pointed look.

"This is *my* coven. I have no lessons to learn, and I already said that I wouldn't tolerate any future transgressions within my home." She glared at Foster. "I'm going to notify the rest of my witches of your arrival, Andie. I'm sorry you were hurt by the spell meant for Foster. I hope you know that you're still safest here, away from uncontrollable beasts that are no longer welcome since they can't obey my very simple rules."

The energy of Foster's body pulsed along my back as we watched Beatrix and the other witches exit the building.

Charlie remained, glancing between Foster and me before her sights stayed on Foster. "You're an alpha?"

"I was. I'm not anymore," Foster replied stiffly.

"You know better than I do that a wolf can't stop being who they were born to be, but I *am* impressed with how well you managed to hide your true power," Charlie said.

Foster said nothing in return. Something told me he wasn't much of a sharer of personal information.

Charlie sighed when she seemed to realize the same thing. "I was wrong about you, Foster. I shouldn't have come at you so harshly when you first showed up. In my defense, I was only trying to protect my best friend from having more hurt in her life."

My lips rose into a smile at the fact that Charlie still thought of me as her best friend. She didn't know me anymore, but I had a feeling that was going to change quickly.

"I would die for Andie. I won't let anyone get away with

threatening or harming her," Foster replied, stepping behind me and wrapping an arm over my chest.

He was possessive, and my body continued to warm from his gestures, but my mind was still muddled. I didn't know him. I hadn't felt an emotional connection to the bond he spoke of, and instant attraction wasn't enough for me to assume he was really my soulmate.

The only reason I hadn't thought Foster was crazy and pushed him away was because Beatrix seemed to believe the same, even if she didn't like him. Plus, there was something in Foster's eyes that drew me to him. He was hurting, and I couldn't stand the thought of furthering that ache in him.

"I don't want to make him leave before I've had the chance to really talk to him," I said to Charlie.

A soft rumble vibrated against my back from Foster. My words had made him happy, which had me fighting another smile.

"Nobody has ever challenged Beatrix inside the coven the way he did," Charlie answered. "I don't think I can help tonight. She probably just needs the night to cool down, and we can figure out a better solution tomorrow."

"If Andie doesn't want me to leave, then that witch isn't going to make me," Foster said.

I'd only been back for a couple of hours, and I was already going to start a war within the home I hadn't realized I'd been missing.

Okay, maybe not a *war*, but still, I didn't like being the cause of discontent. With my memories back, I was eager to see what I'd missed and get to know the people I'd left behind. I couldn't do that if things kept going in this direction.

"You guys can use my house to at least say goodbye or

whatever. I'll take you there and then go see just how pissed Beatrix really is," she added.

"Thanks, Charlie," I replied.

She nodded and headed toward the door.

I turned toward Foster. "Is that okay with you?"

I'd made an assumption when I accepted Charlie's offer that Foster would be fine with some time alone with me based on how he'd been acting, but Beatrix had infuriated him. Maybe he needed some time alone. I didn't want to make this all about me.

He blinked, and some of the darkness left his eyes. "I'm here for you, Andie. No other reason. Whatever you need is what I'll give you."

Jesus, that was intense. I wondered if that made him feel powerless, to be so enveloped by a bond that suddenly made me his sole purpose. I couldn't fathom feeling that way. Being consumed by someone else so completely. Especially not someone I'd just met, which was exactly why I wasn't sure my feelings of attraction had anything to do with the bond. They seemed insignificant compared to the way Foster spoke to me with such conviction.

Clearly, I had a lot to figure out in the coming days without completely losing my mind.

Foster followed me out the door, and Charlie was waiting for us. Her amber eyes were full of concern, and I tried not to wonder why, mostly because there were too many possible reasons.

Instead, I focused on our surroundings. The coven had small cobblestone streets with handfuls of structures on each side, where most of the members stayed, Charlie told me. Not all of the houses looked occupied, but they were all built similarly with painted siding and stone accents, only varying in color and the décor they kept on their doors.

After a few more turns, we stepped onto a street right from my memories. I paused and closed my eyes. I knew that three houses down on the left was where Aunt Junie used to live, a navy-blue home with river rocks surrounding the front door and a covered porch where we used to have picnics together.

Grief of all the time I missed with her was trying to drown me, but I forced myself to continue taking steps forward. I opened my eyes to find Charlie with tears in her own, as if she knew exactly what I'd been thinking, given she'd often taken part in those picnics.

"When I was ready to move out of my parents' house and found out a house on this street was available, I knew I had to have it," Charlie said softly, adding, "It's right across from Junie's still-empty house. I'm sure Beatrix will give it to you if you want."

I hated that I had to even ask this, but since she'd brought them up… "Are your parents still around?"

Charlie nodded. "They're excited to see you again, but I asked them to wait until you were more settled."

As much as I wished to see them as well, Charlie had made the right choice. A little time to get my bearings wasn't a bad thing.

Foster was a couple of feet behind us, and I appreciated that he'd given me some space to have that shared moment with Charlie.

The more time passed, the more I realized his closeness was going to be a lot for me to handle. I needed to consider what that meant without hurting his feelings, and I needed to be careful of my choices or assumptions. I didn't want to make the wrong decision just because I didn't have all the information.

We approached Charlie's cottage. It was sage green with stone siding covering the bottom third of the home. She opened the door but didn't enter.

"There's water, tea, and coffee in the kitchen right on the counter. I'll be back in a bit," she said.

My arms wrapped around her without thinking. "Thank you, Char."

She stiffened before squeezing me twice as hard in return. "Always."

We parted, and I stepped inside with Foster right behind me. He closed the door, and I inhaled the sweet, woodsy scent of the home. The left wall was covered in cedar planks, and small, clear vases of purple flowers were placed throughout the open area and the mantle of the fireplace.

The modest kitchen was straight ahead, and I spotted the coffee maker and tea bags. I headed there first, passing by the living room with several bookshelves and two loveseats.

Wooden floors creaked as Foster followed me. He took a seat on a stool at the counter while I grabbed a cup from the cabinet above the coffee maker.

"Would you like anything?" I offered while putting the tea bag in the empty mug.

"No, thank you."

His eyes were calmer, but there was a tension in his shoulders that I hadn't noticed lessen since I'd first seen him. Something told me that was the permanent set of his rigid muscles.

"I don't really know where to start," I said while I set my mug under the spout and found the button for hot water only.

Foster rubbed a hand over his neck. "I'm sorry if I upset you with my actions earlier."

"With Beatrix? Not really. I mean, it was unexpected, but she'd tried to hurt you."

His throat growled. "Instead, she hurt you. I wanted to kill her, but I didn't think you'd forgive me for that."

I laughed and immediately felt bad when his eyes darkened. "I'm sorry. This is a lot for me. I wish I understood how you felt. Don't get me wrong. I do feel *something*. I mean, look at you."

My lips parted, and I took a deep breath, letting my gaze roam over his long hair, the sexy scruff covering the lower half of his face, and the tattoos marking his thick arms, accented by the fitted black shirt he wore. If this man didn't scream sex appeal, I didn't know what did.

Foster's chest rose and fell faster as I continued to ogle him. "Please stop."

A flush rose to my cheeks, and I turned back to the coffee maker, covering my mouth as I muttered, "I'm so sorry."

The stool scraped across the floor, and I knew he was getting up. Only, I wasn't sure if that was to leave because I'd made him feel like a sex object, or if it was for something else I didn't yet understand.

Seriously, what was wrong with me? I'd only met him an hour ago, if that. I'd had an appreciation for attractive men before, but never so openly. Maybe this was part of the bond I wasn't certain I could feel, or maybe I was just losing my damn mind. Possibly both.

Foster's hands hovered over my arms, his heat seeping through my long sleeves and straight to my core. "That wasn't your fault. It's just...your attraction to me, my wolf can sense it, and it's a lot for us to handle."

"'Us'?" I questioned.

He moved closer to my ear, sending chills down my spine, and speaking softly. "I consider my wolf a part of me. Sometimes it's easier for me to refer to us as the same person. Sometimes not. He's always been with me."

I turned around to face him and found him much nearer than I'd expected. Our chests were practically touching, and I did my best to think about naked old ladies and not about how much I wanted to trail my fingers over his muscled body.

"I'm going to wait in the living room while you finish with your drink," Foster said when I stared dumbfounded at him.

He walked away before I could say anything else, and I wanted to die right there in the kitchen. My lack of sex life since moving to Montana was catching up with me. I needed to find a way to keep my hormones in check or I was going to have more to add to the list of crap going wrong in my life after tonight.

10

FOSTER

Walking away from Andie was painful, but I knew if I didn't, I was going to do something that would end up pushing her away. Even if she tended to look at me like I was a piece of meat—something I wasn't really opposed to—I didn't want her to regret a single moment with me because things were too rushed.

The longer we were around each other, the more I was drawn to her. The need to touch her, protect her, and just be there for her was more than anything I'd ever known.

The strength of the pull frightened the hell out of me if I thought about it too hard. I'd already lost so much, given up so much to prevent myself from ever being vulnerable again. Yet, I was incapable of keeping Andie at a distance.

When she'd merely been an idea of a person, it had been easy to not care as much. To not be excited about the prospect of meeting her because I hadn't truly wanted to. No longer could I go back and pretend I didn't want to give her every part of me.

I tried to warn you, my wolf said quietly.

He had, but I hadn't been willing to listen before. I hadn't wanted to admit I was going to have to care for someone again. That I was going to open myself to the risk of losing the most important thing in the world to me.

I'd already failed my pack and family. The thought of failing Andie… That was unfathomable.

We won't fail her. There's a reason we're here, my wolf added.

I hope you're right.

Andie hadn't freaked out while talking about us being mates, but I knew reality would begin to set in for her soon enough. Right now, she was probably running on the high of returning to where she was born and, from the sounds of it, having cherished memories restored.

Once that wore off, I worried she wasn't going to be as open to having me around. Except I didn't know how to turn off my need to be near her, especially after learning there was a dark witch after my mate.

Hearing Beatrix talk about her "contingency plans" that she didn't want to share had snapped a primal urge inside me, then when she'd hurt Andie instead of me? All I'd been able to see was red.

We made the right choice not harming the witch, my wolf said.

I know, but that doesn't make Beatrix's actions acceptable.

Agreed, but like you said before, we need these witches if we're going to stay close to Andie.

My wolf was right, but he also wasn't being as helpful as I'd hoped. Wolf spirits lived many lifetimes, and mine was on his third. Given the centuries of experience he was supposed to possess, I hadn't thought he'd be so easily distracted. Yet, the moment we'd scented Andie's arousal, the mental images we'd both concocted had made me want to strip her naked and press her against the wall until I'd had my fill.

My dick twitched at the imagery still running rampant in my head, but I shut that down. Andie wasn't just any female. She would be cherished and respected and…

Ours, my wolf finished.

That, I agreed with.

We can't lose control with her, I said.

Things will get easier once she feels the connection as well, he replied.

If *she does*.

My wolf didn't respond to my negativity, but I was glad to end the conversation when I heard something clatter in the kitchen.

"Shit," Andie muttered, and I was on my feet before I could think twice.

When I arrived in the kitchen, she was opening the freezer and red welts were appearing on her forearm. I glanced back at the counter to find the cup of tea she'd been preparing on its side and steaming water dripping onto the floor. Assuming she'd burned herself, I guided her away from the freezer and toward the sink.

"I need an icepack. It burns," she said, trying to fight against me.

"The burning is exactly why you shouldn't use an icepack. You need cool water. Anything too cold could further damage your tissues, assuming you don't rapidly heal on your own."

The witches I'd known had to use a healing spell if they were hurt, but I knew there were ones who existed with powers beyond the normal, just like any other supernatural race's exceptional members. Given Andie's ancestors were from one of the founding families, it was possible she was more special than any of us realized.

"Oh." Andie stopped trying to pull away from me and I got her arm under the running water. She winced, then asked, "How do you know that?"

"Something I read once." I didn't look my age, thanks to my wolf genes, but I'd had a lot of time on my hands during my forty-five years on Earth. Particularly over the last decade. Reading random books had seemed like a good way to keep myself distracted from the anguish that riddled my mind. When fiction had become too much for me with all of its happy endings, I'd switched to medical and historical reads. At least I knew all those hours hadn't been a complete waste of my time.

"Thank you," Andie said once she'd begun to relax under my hold. "If you're sticking around, you'll find I'm somewhat prone to accidents."

My eyes went to her face. Her rosy cheeks were brighter than they'd been before, and her gaze was avoiding mine.

I lifted a hand and pushed her head up. "I meant what I said, Andie. I'm not going anywhere unless you ask me to. I know this is a lot, and you haven't really processed things yet, but out of everything you've learned tonight, I hope you can believe me."

Her lips were tempting when I looked down on her, but I forced myself to keep my focus on her eyes. She was so small in my arms, so unprepared for the world she was returning to. If she asked me to leave, I wasn't sure what I would do. I needed to be the one to prepare her for whatever was to come.

"When I woke up this morning, if I'd known what was coming, I don't think I would have gotten out of bed," she said with a small laugh, then yawned. "Which I'm realizing was a really long time ago."

Andie's head leaned against my chest, and she closed her eyes. She might not have admitted to feeling the bond yet, but there was something there that allowed her to trust me just enough for the moment. That would be enough until we could figure out the rest.

"I really wanted to ask more about this bond, but I don't think I'm going to be able to stay awake much longer," she murmured while I continued to hold her arm under the cool water.

The swelling was already going down, so I turned off the faucet and reached for a towel.

Andie's eyes fluttered open as I dried her off. "You enjoy taking care of people."

"Just you," I replied.

She shook her head and loosely ran her other hand down her front. "I get this tingly sensation that runs through my body every time I witness someone doing something with real passion. I know what I'm talking about."

Her voice was strong and certain, the complete opposite from the tiredness she'd just been displaying. I wanted to argue with her, just to see if I could rile her, but she also wasn't wrong.

I might have denied my alpha side for my own selfish reasons, but that didn't change who I was at the core. Though, I'd learned long ago that it was better to be alone than to try to pretend to be someone else around others.

If I wasn't going to be alone any longer, I wasn't going to

try to convince Andie that she was wrong. She deserved better than that from me.

"Let's get you to bed," I said instead of getting further into a conversation she wasn't ready for when she was dead on her feet.

Andie nodded, letting me guide her to the hallway. There were only two doors: a bathroom on the left and a bedroom on the right, which I assumed was where Charlie planned to sleep.

"Charlie won't mind sharing," she said, pulling away from me and heading into the room.

I stood at the doorway, eyeing the two windows and making sure they were locked. "When you're ready to talk tomorrow, just come outside of the barrier if Beatrix is still pissed. I won't be far."

Andie leaned against the bed with widened eyes. "You're not going to sleep out there, are you?"

I smirked. "I'm a wolf shifter, Andie. It's not anything we haven't done plenty of times before."

"That's not normal."

"Not for you. For me and my wolf, it is."

I didn't want to leave her, but there was a very small part of me that was glad she wasn't asking me to stay. Time apart for us to think would do us both some good. I knew without a doubt in my mind that I wanted Andie, but my need for her couldn't overshadow what was best for her. Both were reasons why I was willing to leave the coven without being sure that Beatrix would let me back in. Andie was going to need her coven to survive just as much as I hoped she'd need me one day soon.

I had to keep that at the forefront of my thoughts before I lost her, too.

Andie started to sway on the bed, her eyes barely staying open. I stepped onto the carpeted floor and closed the distance between us in three strides. Gently, I placed one hand over her cheek and kissed the other.

"Sleep well, Andie."

Ignoring the widening of her eyes when my lips touched her skin, I forced myself to leave the room and headed for the front door. Every step was harder than the last, but this was the right move.

I opened the door and twisted the lock on the interior handle before pulling it closed. When I turned around, Charlie was standing there with what seemed like an accusatory raised brow.

"Leaving so soon?" she asked.

"I don't want to fight with you or Beatrix. That's not what Andie needs," I said.

She sighed. "I wasn't prepared to share her once I got her back."

"She's my mate," I replied simply yet sternly.

Charlie waved a hand in the air. "Yeah, I know. Listen, I'm sorry. Again. You don't know what it's been like. Andie was the sister I never had. Her family was my family. When her dad died and they left, I lost more than a piece of me that day. I was banned from ever going after her until Junie died, then it was too late. Or so we'd thought. Andie's in trouble, and I realize she's going to need all of us to protect her."

"Who is this Moira witch?" I asked.

"Someone we should have dealt with a long time ago. She's dangerous and not to be taken lightly."

"So am I." I growled.

Charlie took a step toward her door, passing by me. "Maybe you'll be just what we need to beat her, then."

"Are you saying this coven isn't enough to protect Andie from what's coming?" I asked.

"I'm saying there's a reason Beatrix hasn't stopped Moira before. We can beat her, but at what cost? We don't know. It hasn't been a gamble worth taking until now. Beatrix won't willingly give over Andie. She'll fight to the death for her, but we're all aware this battle won't be without great loss."

"Then maybe your coven shouldn't have waited so long to act, regardless of the risks, and none of this would be happening."

"Maybe not, but then maybe Andie wouldn't have ever made her way back here. We'll never know, and I won't live my life based on *maybe*s and *what if*s."

The witch was making a point, but I had my own ideas to consider.

"I'll be back by sunrise. Make sure Andie remembers I'll be waiting beyond the barrier once she's awake," I said.

Charlie nodded and headed inside as I turned back the way I'd entered the coven. After that chat, I knew there was something else I had to do before Andie woke up.

We're going to the pack, my wolf said.

I won't let my past be the reason Andie is vulnerable.

It was late, but Holden always said I could come by anytime, and I didn't doubt his sincerity. I was going to ask for his help, even if that meant I had to join his pack, something I'd sworn I wouldn't do. But that was before everything changed.

Witches peeked out of their windows when I passed, but I paid them no attention as I began running toward the edge of the barrier. It was after midnight, and while I hoped Andie would get as much rest as she needed, I wanted to be back early in case she had a hard time sleeping.

I leaped over the gate we'd come through and shifted midair once we were outside the barrier.

The pack was southeast of the coven, and we sprinted that way, lengthening our stride as long as it would go.

My wolf howled, signaling to the others we were headed their way. Holden would no doubt have guards out, and I didn't want to chance them thinking we were coming for a fight.

They should recognize our scent when we get closer, my wolf said.

Doesn't mean they'll be welcoming if they don't know why we're suddenly showing up.

Everything will be fine, he added.

It was a gamble to tell Holden who I really was. Or who I'd been. He'd said he knew about my past, but did he know the whole story? I'd never allowed our conversations to go deep enough to find out.

He didn't seem overly territorial, but I'd never accepted his offer of going inside his pack. He might have been a better actor than I'd suspected, and I could be making a mistake in trusting him, but I didn't feel like we had any other option at this point.

Plus, having Holden on our side could help with Beatrix. The old witch seemed to like the alpha from what I'd seen the first time they cornered me together. I'd use whatever advantage I could to stay close to Andie.

It wasn't long before we entered wolf territory. Eyes watched us from the trees, but nobody came closer when we found the main gravel road leading to the pack. The trees around us were dense, and the only light came from the moon and stars above until porchlights flickered up ahead.

There was a massive log house at the end of the road. It

was two stories with tree trunks holding up a second-story porch and a massive A-frame-style main window at the center of the home.

Holden was waiting for me at the front door. He nodded when I met his stare, and I shifted back to my human form.

"I didn't think I'd be seeing you so soon, Foster," he said as I approached.

"Neither did I, but things have changed."

He raised a brow. "You found that mate of yours?"

"I did, and she needs help. More than I'm worried I can give her on my own," I admitted regrettably.

Holden gestured to the door, then the porch chairs. "Then let's talk. Wherever you're comfortable at."

The alpha knew me better than I'd realized, and I wasn't sure how I felt about that.

"I can't stay for too long, so out here is fine." I took a seat on one of the wooden chairs, expecting the hard surface to be uncomfortable, but was surprised by its smoothness.

Holden sat next to me. "What happened?"

"My mate is a witch, as we suspected earlier. Since she's part of one of the founding covens, there's another witch that wants her power, and Andie, my mate, was attacked tonight. I'm sure there's more, but I had a disagreement with Beatrix and didn't get all of the information. Though, this was enough to know I needed help."

Holden chuckled, deeper wrinkles forming around his green eyes. "A disagreement? Right. What did you do?"

"I didn't hurt the old witch, but she now knows something I'm not sure you do. Considering I'm asking for your help in keeping my mate safe, I feel I owe you full disclosure."

Holden leaned forward on his elbow and clasped his

hands. "I already know who you are, Foster. I tried to tell you before. Do you think I'd let a rogue wolf stay in my territory for this long without having done my research? I just never pushed you to talk because you weren't ready. Even now, you don't need to explain yourself to me."

A sigh of relief left me, even though I was annoyed he'd been able to figure out my past, but I let him continue without asking how he'd learned about me.

"I also know you don't want to be a part of my pack and I get why, but I need you to reconsider joining us. I can't ask my family to fight for your mate if you're not one of us. We recently lost some of our own in a battle that wasn't ours to be involved in, but one that would have made things more difficult for supernaturals as a whole if the outcome hadn't gone the way we'd wanted. I can't ask them to do that again so soon without it directly benefiting our pack."

I'd known joining his pack was going to be a requirement, and I was prepared to move past my personal issues if it meant keeping Andie as safe as possible.

"I can make a commitment to your pack as long as you understand that my mate comes first and she's not one of us. I won't pretend otherwise, and I know that's not fair of me to ask for your help when I can't promise I'll be able to reciprocate for the long term, but that's the way things are right now."

Holden nodded, offering me an understanding smile. "I like your honesty, Foster, and I have a feeling this will work out better than either of us know. I accept your limitations, not only because of your mate, but because of your past. Maybe this is just what you need to heal. Not only for yourself, but for your wolf, too. Being alone all these years isn't good for either of you."

"Spoken like a true alpha," I replied.

He clasped my shoulder. "Let's make things official. I'll grab my beta, and we'll do this quietly. Tomorrow, I'll inform the pack, and I expect you to formally introduce yourself within the next two days."

"Not a problem. Thank you, Holden."

"We all deserve a second chance in life. I hope you can find yours here."

My lips downturned, and I rubbed the back of my neck. I wasn't sure Holden was right, but now that I'd found Andie, I at least had something to fight for. That was more than I'd had in a long time.

11

When I woke up, the sky was still dark, and Charlie was sitting on the bed staring at me.

"Hi." She grinned and waved.

"What time is it?" I asked as I sat up, trying not to be creeped out by how cheery she was.

Charlie tapped the screen on her phone. "Almost five."

"Have you slept at all?" She was still dressed in the same clothes, but so was I, so that didn't mean much.

"Nah. I gave myself a boost of energy so I could keep watch. We've got some curious witches. People who remember you and your mom from before. I didn't want anyone coming over unannounced and scaring the hell out of you."

"So, you sat watch over me like a stalker instead?" I joked.

She nodded. "Pretty much. Did you sleep okay? You were practically unconscious when I walked in right after Foster left."

I covered my face with my hands and groaned. "I'd

wanted to talk to him, figure out what this mate thing really means to him and set some boundaries, but I was so deliriously tired that I ended up hurting myself and snuggling with him at your sink. He probably thinks I'm crazy."

Charlie laughed. "I'm not sure how you snuggle at the sink, but please explain."

I told her about my tea mishap and the burn and how Foster had stopped me from making things worse.

She chuckled. "Oh, that's amazing. I wish I'd been here to see it. I wasn't sure about Foster at first, but I'm beginning to see he really does care about you. Not many people have the tits to challenge Beatrix."

I raised a brow. "'The tits', huh?"

"Yep, but in all seriousness, I'm glad you have him and that I have you back. Even though we've both changed since the last time we really knew each other, I meant it when I said I hadn't forgotten or replaced you." Charlie reached behind her, grabbed a picture frame from her nightstand, and handed it to me.

It was the two of us on the tire swing that had been in my backyard. We were soaking wet from the rain and laughing. The day had been maybe a month before I'd left with my mother.

"I wish I'd known," I whispered.

Charlie reached for me. "Your mother made the best choice she could at the time. Maybe it wasn't the right one, but I'm a firm believer in everything happening for a reason. We can't change what happened then, so I don't want to waste time dwelling on it. We have more important things to discuss."

At least Charlie and I had grown up with likeminded

outlooks on life. While I'd thought I might grow to resent my mother for taking me from here, I was coming around to the idea that maybe it had been for the best. I'd gotten as much time with her as I could before she'd died. Who knew how my life would have turned out if we'd stayed? It might have been better, but it also could have been worse, and I was glad it hadn't been.

"Would Moira be the more important thing we need to discuss?" I asked.

"Yes and no. Moira wants your magic, but you don't exactly have it. We need to figure out how to lift the block Junie helped you create."

I took a deep breath. Okay, maybe I wasn't *completely* handling everything as well as I had been the night before.

Charlie's hand covered my bouncing knee. "Do you want me to help you relax?"

My eyes widened. "Is that what happened last night?"

Charlie grimaced. "Well, I didn't do it, but Beatrix might have given you a little something extra when she unlocked your memories to keep you from storming off again. The experience can be pretty overwhelming otherwise."

I drummed my fingers over my crossed arms. Beatrix had given me a gift but then stolen my true emotions. She was too devious for her own good, and I was going to make sure she knew her little tricks weren't okay with me the next time I saw her.

"Does she realize I made a fool out of myself with Foster because of my lack of inhibitions? I mean, *a soulmate*? Why wasn't I freaking out about that?" Now that I'd asked the question, my palms became sweaty, and my heart raced as I struggled to take even shallow breaths.

Charlie grabbed both of my shoulders. "Calm down,

Andie. What Beatrix did to you wasn't anything that made you feel something you wouldn't have already had stirring inside you. Yes, she took away any uneasiness you would have had after remembering everything you did and learning about Foster, but the rest was all you. Any feelings you expressed with actions were your own."

"Still, Beatrix had no right to do that without my permission."

"You're right, she didn't, but remember? We aren't dwelling on the past." Charlie smirked, and I rolled my eyes. I wouldn't exactly consider six hours ago the past. Regardless, I let it go for the time being and brought up another important subject.

"I do have a question about the mate thing, though." I placed my hand over my sprinting heart. "I don't feel anything here. Sure, I find Foster attractive, and his growls are hot, and the way he's so damn protective is straight out of every woman's dream, but shouldn't there be more? I feel like I'm missing something regarding this whole soulmate situation."

"That's because you are, and I think that's due to your magic being constricted. Beatrix was able to mess with your mind, but the heart is a much different story and that's where our magic generates from. We need you to remember the spell you and Junie used. Knowing her and how much she cared about you, she would have made it special. Do you remember a moment standing out more than the others around the time you last saw her?

I thought back to the last day Aunt Junie had made an appearance. It had been at my birthday party. She'd been so sad when I'd hugged her. I hadn't understood why then, but knowing what she'd had to do, her darkened emotions made more sense.

I closed my eyes and tried harder to recall the details of that day. I'd been wearing a green dress and had on a purple crown that read, "Birthday Girl" in bright pink letters. As I searched deeper, I sucked in a breath and my body went rigid.

Aunt Junie was at the door, holding a gift bag. There were tears in her eyes and her smile didn't reach her eyes like normal.

I ran to her, wrapping my arms around her waist. "Aunt Junie!"

"Hi, my little dragon. Happy birthday." She rubbed a hand over my then-dark red hair.

I tugged on her free hand, wanting to show her my cake. "Come on. You gotta see what Momma got me."

My mother was there. She was stiff and off to the side but watching us intently.

Aunt Junie kneeled to my level. "I'm afraid I can't stay long. I just came to bring you a gift and say goodbye." A lone tear shed down her cheek.

I wiped it away, sticking my lower lip out. "Where are you going?"

"I have to go away for work, but I couldn't leave without saying goodbye to my most favorite person in the world. Would you mind opening your present before I leave?"

At her mention of a present, I brightened, not understanding the severity of what was happening.

I nodded and followed Aunt Junie into the sitting room with my mom right behind us. Aunt Junie pulled a small wooden box from the gift bag she had and held it out for me.

My little fingers flipped the golden latch and gently pulled the lid up. Inside was the prettiest stone I'd ever seen. Shaped like a teardrop in a shiny white color with glints of blue reflecting off the surface as I moved it around.

"Can I wear it?" I asked excitedly.

Aunt Junie shook her head. "Not until you're older, but I do need you to hold it for me."

She took the box from me and carefully pulled the necklace out, resting the stone in one hand and the long, silver chain in her other.

"It's glowing. Just like me," I whispered to her, knowing that I wasn't supposed to tell anyone what I could do sometimes.

"That's right, little dragon. This is special. Just like you. And I want you to keep it with you always." She placed the warming stone in my palm and wrapped her hands over mine. "Repeat after me, okay?"

I nodded, thinking that we were going to do one of the special tricks I was only allowed to do with Aunt Junie.

"Celarius navatio, conservus sempra. Afuro malis, servo sempra. Abscondi supremius."

The words rolled from my tongue fluidly, even though I had no idea what they meant and had never heard them before. We chanted them over and over until my chest burned and tears fell from my eyes. I tried to pull away, but Aunt Junie wouldn't let me, even though she cried harder than I did.

By the time we were done, I was wailing, and she enveloped me in her arms. "I'm so sorry, Andie. I love you so much. I hope you always remember how special you are to me and how strong you are. Always my little dragon."

She placed her hand over my forehead and chest. My skin warmed, and the pain I'd just been feeling disappeared along with what we'd just done.

My mother approached with open arms and wet cheeks. She

softly thanked Aunt Junie, barely able to meet her eyes as she took me into her arms.

Aunt Junie said nothing in reply. Instead, a painful sound left her mouth, and she exited the house in a scrambling hurry.

Just like that, Aunt Junie was gone, along with the sadness I no longer remembered I should be feeling.

My eyes opened and my soul ached when I came out of the memory. I wrapped my arms around myself, rocking back and forth. Aunt Junie had spelled me to forget the worst of her departure. She'd taken my feelings with her and carried them all on her own until she'd died.

Charlie's hand rubbed over my back while I regained my composure. "You were muttering words I didn't fully hear. What did you remember?"

"I heard the spell we did. I don't think she blocked my magic. I think she put it in a moonstone necklace."

"Shit. Of course, she did. Where's the necklace?" Charlie asked, looking around my neck and finding nothing there.

"Back at my house in Montana, along with all of my other belongings. Damn it. I should have listened and been willing to leave with you. If I had, I could have packed that along with all of the other important items I might never get back."

Hysteria was clawing at my chest and working its way up my throat. Everything inside me burned with sorrow for things lost. Sure, I could replace most of them, but not the pictures of me and mom while growing up. Not the necklace that I probably needed more than I realized.

My thoughts ran rampant and thoughts of more things I needed to do surfaced. "And my work. I need to call them and let them know… What am I supposed to tell people?"

My phone hadn't been in working order when I'd tried to order a ride home after leaving work. I wasn't even sure I had the phone numbers I'd need. More panic exploded within, and I could only manage to gasp in short breaths of air.

"I'm so sorry, Andie. I wish we had time for me to hug you and eat all the ice cream, but we don't. We can't wait a second longer to see if your necklace is still in the house." Charlie was texting on her phone, fingers flying over the screen before she continued. "We'll get you a new phone soon and you can tell whoever you need to that there's been a family emergency and you've already left with no intentions of returning, but not until we're done searching your house. Nobody can know that we're going back until we've already left."

I put my hands over my face and sobbed. This was the freak-out I should have had the night before, and it felt twice as worse from being postponed. My shoulders shook and I didn't hold anything back. I needed however many minutes I could have to pour everything out.

Charlie's arms wrapped tightly around me, and she rocked me back and forth. "I wish I could make all of this better for you, Andie. Even more so, I wish we had more time, but we need to go unless you'd rather I went with the others and you stayed here."

I took a shuddering breath and swiped my sleeves over my wet face. "No, I'll be okay. I just needed a minute. Do you think there's any chance the necklace or anything else important is still there?"

Charlie grimaced. "I doubt whoever had shown up when I teleported us out of there merely knocked and left when you didn't answer the door."

Damn it. This was not what I wanted to hear. I should

have been asking all of these questions the moment I'd arrived. I should have done a lot of things, and not just as of last night, but a long time ago, too.

"Where's Beatrix?" I asked.

"She's on her way over here. I already let her know about what you remembered. She's gathering the team she created to search for you now, and we need to go meet them. They'll be coming with us back to your house to search for the necklace."

"And my other things. I have stuff from my mother and memories. I won't give those things up. Not again."

Charlie nodded and slid off the bed. "I'll do whatever I can to make sure we grab as much as possible, but I won't lie. There's a chance we won't have time for anything other than the necklace. It just depends on what we find when we get there."

I wanted to be angry at Charlie's words, but I knew it wasn't her fault that any of this had happened.

She disappeared into a walk-in closet, and I started to make a mental list of all the items I wanted to grab just in case things weren't as bad as Charlie was suspecting. My mom's old photo albums, her jewelry box where I also kept the necklace, a few pictures off the walls, some clothes I could replace but really didn't want to, and maybe even some of the random gifts my mom had given me over the years.

Charlie's golden-blonde hair peeked out from the closet. "Foster is going to be a problem. You'll want to see him before we leave so he knows why you've disappeared."

"How would he know the difference? I could still be sleeping." I wasn't sure I had the mindset to deal with him, especially after how I'd acted the night before. Getting so close to him the way I had and openly being attracted to him when he was a complete stranger wasn't who I was under normal circumstances. I needed to be more in control of myself before I faced him again, and after my little breakdown, I didn't trust that time had arrived yet.

"He's your soulmate and you're his mate. He'll know," Charlie replied before disappearing again.

"But how?" I demanded.

"Magic, Andie. That's the answer for a lot of things around here, even when we don't want it to be."

Of course, it freaking was.

12

ANDIE

The sun came shining through the window while I finished getting dressed. The water droplets left on my exposed skin after my earlier shower warmed before vanishing while I stared outside, adjusting the hem of my borrowed shirt.

Pale yellows mixed with the lavender sky, and the light from the sun began to spread across the horizon, snuffing out the darkness. I closed my eyes and searched deep inside myself, hoping for answers to questions I wasn't even sure how to ask.

Never could I have imagined the energy I'd been trying to ignore would lead to a world like this. One filled with witches, shifters, vampires, and fae. Hell, there might be more out there that I wasn't aware of, but that wasn't something I could think about now. First, I needed to know who I was and what I was going to do about Foster.

Having my memories restored went a long way in preventing me from being in constant freak-out mode, but still, I only had the knowledge of a child when it came to this life. There were still so many unknowns.

If my magic had been locked away in a necklace, how did my hands glow and what did that glow mean? Was the little magic I did have the reason Foster was drawn to me? And how had he known where I was going to be, but not where I'd been? That was something I should have asked during our first meeting, but I blamed Beatrix for my lack of clear thinking the night before.

The longer I stood there, the tighter the knot in my chest became. With my eyes still closed, I tried once more to access the magic within me, but there was nothing other than a gentle warmth filling my core. No tingling sensation and no glow. Those two things only seemed to appear when they wanted to.

There was a soft knock on the door to Charlie's bedroom before it creaked open. She popped her head inside and grinned. "Good call on rolling the jeans up. Other than them being a little long on you, everything looks like it fits."

I nodded. "Thanks again for the clothes."

"Beatrix is here. She wants to talk before we leave."

With one last gaze at the rising sun, I headed for the living room to meet Beatrix, hoping she was going to apologize for being so rude to Foster and what she did to me. Though, the hope was more than likely futile.

After only a couple of hours around them both, I already knew they were too much alike. Nothing about interacting with them was going to be easy, but a girl could still hope.

Beatrix sat on Charlie's couch with her ankles crossed and shoulders back. She stared at the pictures on the wall. Her face was tense, but her eyes were soft until she turned toward me.

The older witch appraised me and tsked. "We have to make you less *human*. It's not right seeing you without your magic."

"I'm not sure how I'm supposed to respond to that," I said, glancing at Charlie.

"You don't," Charlie muttered, bringing a smirk to Beatrix's lips.

Beatrix stood and came closer to me. I was ready to dash to the right when I saw her hand twitch, but Charlie held me in place.

"She's more bark than bite when it comes to coven members. Don't get me wrong, her bite is wicked, but you can trust her," Charlie whispered.

"You'd do well to listen to Charlotte. I've been watching her, and she's becoming quite the witch. Though I won't soon forget she went to Montana without telling me first," Beatrix said, briefly narrowing her gaze on Charlie, who groaned, likely from the use of her given name.

When we'd been about four, she'd hated that I had a boyish name and hers was so proper. Against her mother's wishes, my best friend had somehow convinced nearly everyone in our coven to call her "Charlie" instead. When her parents had found out, I remembered her dad being so proud and her mom merely sighing in defeat.

While I appreciated them giving me space to get settled, I was eager to see them again. Maybe after we got back, Charlie could make that happen.

Beatrix stilled when she was within touching distance of me, then continued. "About last night. What do you want to do about that wolf?"

Both of my brows rose. She was *asking* me? I hadn't thought I'd get much of a say.

"I don't know. My gut says that you're telling me the truth about this soulmate thing, but unless I'm wrong in my assumptions about what to expect, I don't feel anything outside of physical attraction. Mostly because of whatever you did to me, which *I* won't soon forget."

When my eyes narrowed at the old witch, she at least had the audacity to avert her gaze from mine.

"That wasn't for Foster's benefit. Believe me. I wanted to make sure you didn't attempt to run off again, and keeping your panic receptors dulled was the best way to do that. Regardless, maybe I was wrong about the wolf. Maybe he's not your soulmate."

There was a pang in my chest when the words left Beatrix's mouth. My hand covered the ache, pressing down, and warmth built in my palms.

I closed my eyes, focusing on the energy. Normally, I did whatever I could think of to make the energy fade away, but not now. I wanted answers, and drawing out whatever was inside me seemed like the only way that I was going to get them.

"Holy shit," Charlie muttered.

I opened my eyes to find a pink glow casting throughout the entire room and Beatrix holding her palms just over my shoulders. As soon as I pulled my hand away from my chest, the light disappeared.

"Interesting. Maybe I wasn't wrong. Pity. We should be going." Beatrix moved away from me and toward the door.

"How can I do whatever that just was if my magic is supposed to be locked in a necklace?" I asked before following her.

Beatrix turned around but left her hand on the door handle. "The majority of your magic is in that necklace. Junie had to leave a small fraction of your energy so you could assist with the spell. That bit is what you've been feeling, but it won't be enough to keep you safe."

Beatrix's answer made sense, but still, I didn't understand. "If I've had magic this whole time, then why couldn't you find me? My mother always knew where I was when we lived here. No matter how hard Charlie and I tried to hide, our parents always found us using a tracking spell."

She sighed and met my eyes. "There aren't always answers to the questions we have, Andie. Don't think that we didn't search for you—because I had my best witches trying to track you. The only conclusion I came to is we weren't meant to find you until it was time."

"Time for what?" I asked quietly.

"That's what we need to figure out." Beatrix opened the door and walked outside without turning back.

I met Charlie's pinched gaze. "I don't like the sound of that."

She nodded. "Neither do I, but you're not alone anymore. Whatever is going to happen, we'll face it together. Just like we used to."

With a deep breath, I took her offered hand and we left her house, heading back toward the courtyard where I'd first met Foster the night before. Being there reminded me that Charlie had suggested I let him know I was leaving, so I mentioned as much to Beatrix when we found her talking to three other witches.

She waved her hand flippantly. "He'll be fine. Plus, he deserves a little panic after the way he acted last night."

"The way *he* acted?" I asked incredulously. "You were going to zap him with magic."

"He first tried to bite me and then raised his voice at me.

He needed to know that isn't acceptable behavior in my coven," she answered, then she pursed her lips. "I am sorry I hit you instead. Does that count?"

There was no sincerity in her apology, but I didn't care about what she'd done to me. My energy had flared when Beatrix had mentioned Foster not being my soulmate. That told me enough to know that he was important. Even if I didn't understand how or why, something inside me wasn't going to let her push him away.

"Sure, it counts. I'm just going to see if Foster's waiting outside like he said. If he is, I'll let him know that I won't be gone long."

"I see you're going to be just as stubborn as your mother." Beatrix sighed, then gestured to the three witches standing beside her. "This is Evelyn, Ava, and Benjamin. They'll be joining us today. Let me finish with them, and then I'll go with you. I need to grant you access to the coven anyway."

"Thank you," I said before appraising the others present. The first one Beatrix had called "Evelyn" I remembered seeing the night before. She was older with hazel eyes and long, white hair that was braided over her shoulder.

The second witch, named Ava, was younger, maybe in her forties with short ebony hair, light-grey eyes, and thin lips that turned down more as Beatrix spoke in hushed tones. She might have also been around the night before, but too much was happening to be sure.

Benjamin, the last one Beatrix had gestured to, was the youngest of the three, appearing more like a teenager than an adult with his round face, curly auburn hair, and pale-blue eyes. There was even a smattering of freckles on his cheeks, adding to his youthfulness.

Charlie turned her back to the group and leaned closer to me, keeping her voice low. "Evelyn has been Beatrix's right-hand woman since we lost Junie. She makes Beatrix look friendly on her worst days, so watch out for her. Ava is chill most of the time unless she's too stressed, then give her a wide berth. Benjamin, I still haven't figured out. His mom kept him out of the public eye for a while, but Beatrix convinced her to let him help look for you since he inherited his dad's tracking abilities."

"Thanks for that." Even though my memories had come back to me clearer than should have been possible, I didn't remember most of the coven. I knew there were dozens of witches and warlocks living here, but most faces were a blur unless they'd specifically interacted with me.

Beatrix rejoined us. "They're going to create a secure portal for us to walk through. It's safer than teleporting, but it will take some time opening. While we wait, we can go see how the wolf enjoyed sleeping on the forest floor."

I had to bite my tongue to keep from snapping at her. Beatrix was supposed to be like family, and I hardly knew the wolf. Her snide comments shouldn't have annoyed me like they did, but I couldn't deny I wanted to stand up for him.

The stone path led to the white wooden gate I remembered going through the night before. As we got closer, I could see a shimmer in front of the fence that I hadn't noticed the first time.

"Give me your hand," Beatrix demanded, holding out her own.

I complied but added, "You know, it wouldn't kill you to be nice."

She raised a brow. "It might. I'd rather not find out."

The snarky witch pressed my hand between both of hers and started muttering. I glanced toward the trees, and the "dog" I'd seen the night before exited from the forest. Only he wasn't a dog.

In my previously panicked state, I'd mistaken a massive wolf for a house pet. I wasn't sure how I'd done that, but I could only assume that my mind had processed him as something normal to keep me from spiraling further.

The onyx-colored wolf stalked forward, bright-blue eyes staring directly at me. I sucked in a breath, and my body stiffened.

Charlie nudged me with a grin on her face. "Bond or not, that wolf has your number. He can't see us, but he certainly *sees* you."

Shivers ran down my spine, and I couldn't tear my eyes away from the ginormous animal. He had to be close to four feet tall and probably weighed more than a couple hundred pounds under all of his dark, thick fur.

The wolf stopped, and the air shimmered around him before his head dipped down, then I blinked and Foster was standing there, fully dressed in jeans and a dark grey T-shirt, still staring right at me.

"How?" I asked, hoping Charlie was still next to me, even though I hadn't turned back to her.

"As I said before, the answer is almost always magic, Andie. Even wolves have their own kind, gifted to them from their creator, the Moon Goddess."

I took a step closer to the barrier, but Beatrix yanked on my arm, reminding me I was supposed to be paying attention to her.

"Move again and this is going to hurt a lot more," she grumbled.

Just as I was about to ask *what* was going to hurt, shock traveled up my arm and over my chest, then spread through the rest of my body. My spine straightened, and I gritted my teeth, staying as still as possible.

The current running through me lasted only a few seconds, but that was enough to know I didn't want to do that again. Not ever.

"You can come and go as you please now, but you can't bring anyone inside with you without another coven member's help," Beatrix said before grimacing at Foster.

"You don't trust me?" I asked with a bite in my voice.

She rolled her eyes. "We have a lot to learn about each other, Andie. If I didn't trust you, you wouldn't be here at all. You need magic to give someone else permission to enter. That's the same for any witch here."

Oh. That made sense. I felt bad for snapping at her, but she'd brought it on herself. The witch seemed proud of her lack of niceties.

Beatrix exited the barrier when I didn't say anything else. I followed with Charlie at my side. As soon as I stepped through, Foster started to raise his hands as if to reach out to me, but then quickly tucked them behind his back.

"Did you get enough rest?" he asked, his eyes traveling over my body.

I nodded with a small smile on my face and tried to ignore the heat unfurling inside me. "I did, and I'd like to continue our conversation, but I came to let you know it will have to wait a bit. We're going back to my house to grab some things. Charlie mentioned you might know I was gone and that I should give you a heads-up."

"I'll come with you," he said, then he finally looked at Beatrix, who was already shaking her head.

"Absolutely not. You can't be controlled," she said.

A rumble grew in Foster's chest. "*My* control shouldn't be the one in question."

"How about your snapping jaws? Your lack of respect for authority? Or your anger? Or a litany of other things I could name off, but we don't have time for that. This was a courtesy, Foster. Don't make me regret it. We'll be back in five minutes." Beatrix turned her back on him, but he reached out and grabbed her wrist.

"I can't let her go to the place she was just attacked at without my protection. I'm coming with you," he growled.

Shit. I hadn't thought he'd be that protective of me. I didn't know what to do, but I couldn't just stand there.

I stepped between them, once again choosing to act at the exact wrong time.

Beatrix's palm shoved into my chest, and I was on my ass in the next second.

13

FOSTER

A snarl ripped from my chest as I shoved Beatrix back. I told myself the night before that I wouldn't threaten her again, that I would do whatever was best for Andie, but I didn't expect her to tell me they were leaving.

The idea that Andie could be in danger and I wouldn't be there to keep her safe made me snap. With the bond there, but not fully intact, I wasn't myself. Add that to the fact that I'd willingly joined a pack that wasn't going to let me fade into the background, and I was more on edge than I'd been in years.

"She isn't safe with you," I roared at Beatrix after she once again hit my mate with unnecessary magic. I bent down, scooping Andie up, and held her tightly against me, as if my mere touch would make everything better.

"If you'd quit acting like a caveman, Andie wouldn't have gotten hurt. Either time," Beatrix spat.

"You're trying to keep her from me, and I won't let you," I said, then glanced down at Andie.

She was shaking, and her eyes were squeezed shut. I shifted my hold on her and used one of my hands to cup her cheek. "Can you hear me, Andie?"

She didn't respond, and I sneered at Beatrix. "What did you do to her?"

"Move so I can fix it," she said, stepping closer, but I didn't trust the witch.

"Not a chance in hell."

Beatrix's hands curled into fists, and I turned Andie away from her in case the crazy witch tried to do anything else reckless.

Charlie stepped forward, hands up in surrender. "Foster, give me Andie. You know I won't hurt her."

I wanted to believe the golden-haired witch, but letting Andie go was proving harder than I'd thought it would be.

She's ours to protect, my wolf said. Just when I thought he was agreeing with my choice to keep Andie to myself, he added, *But Beatrix is fighting for the same thing we are.*

No, she's not. She keeps hurting Andie.

On accident and you know it.

Accident or not, Beatrix can't be trusted.

I wasn't going to give my mate over to her again.

What about Charlie? She loves Andie. You can feel the concern coming from her, my wolf said.

I glanced back at Charlie. She was inching closer while Beatrix stood behind her, staring daggers at me.

Andie whimpered in my arms. She was hurting, and I wasn't going to make her better on my own. *Damn it!*

I stepped toward Charlie and carefully handed Andie over, but Charlie asked me to hold her up instead of letting go.

I moved my hands to rest under Andie's arms, and she twitched in my hold. "Hurry," I demanded of Charlie.

She placed her hands over Andie's chest and winced, then glanced back at Beatrix. "That was low, even for you."

Beatrix didn't respond, not even with a scowl as her eyes stayed on Andie.

Dark puffs of smoke rose from Andie's chest, and when Charlie pulled her hand back, there were scorch marks on her palm.

"She's going to be okay now," Charlie said softly, taking a step back.

"Take her," I said to Charlie.

She reached out, grabbing Andie just as she began to stir. I wanted my face to be the first thing Andie saw when she came to, but I also had a witch to teach a lesson to. Beatrix couldn't keep acting the way she was. Andie was mine and she knew it.

I took two steps toward Beatrix before she held glowing silver hands up. "Touch me again and I will force you into your wolf form for the rest of your days."

"Stand down, Foster." Holden's alpha power rolled over me, and my steps faltered.

I turned to see him coming out of the trees, breathing hard as if he'd sprinted all the way here.

"She hurt Andie. Again," I said, glaring at the smirking witch.

"And we'll talk about that, but that doesn't give you the right to hurt Beatrix in return. If you truly want to help Andie, you'll find a way to work with her coven leader," Holden said.

Just as I was about to snarl at him for taking the witch's side, he faced Beatrix. "And you should be ashamed of yourself as a leader, Beatrix. You know their connection. We've even talked about what it would mean should one of your witches be his mate. I don't know what games you're playing, but they need to end. Now."

Beatrix straightened, losing her smirk. "As much as I'd hate to continue this conversation, we really do have somewhere to be and Foster can't come. Andie's magic could be in danger of landing in the wrong hands. Once we have it, we can resume discussing this unfortunate circumstance."

Holden clasped my shoulder, but his hold no longer contained me. "Are you saying Andie doesn't have her magic?"

My voice was devoid of emotion. I'd suspected there was something wrong with Andie's magic thanks to my wolf, but given that she'd glowed pink, I didn't think she was without it. This information changed things drastically.

"It's complicated, but essentially yes. That's how she survived hiding amongst the humans for so long. Now, we need to go," Beatrix answered.

I wanted to argue, but Holden whispered in my ear. "Give them this. Show them you can be reasonable. Andie needs you to do that."

Damn him for being right. I turned to Andie, needing reassurance that she was okay. She was standing with Charlie, and there was still a slight shake in her hands.

"I'm sorry," I said while closing the distance between us.

"That was nothing. I'm fine." She was lying, but I wasn't going to call her on it.

"Do you want to go with them?" I asked.

"I do. I'll let you know as soon as we're back."

Staring into her soft blue eyes, I knew she was telling the

truth. She wasn't trying to leave me. Otherwise, she wouldn't have even told me she was going.

Fuck. The bond was stronger than I'd realized. I wasn't thinking right, but I didn't know what to do to fix things.

"Be safe," I said, then took a step back.

Charlie helped Andie back across the barrier, and they disappeared together. All I could see in front of me now were trees, but Andie's presence was strong. I could feel her in my soul, even through the witch's shield. I knew when she was getting farther away and when she paused, hopefully looking back at me.

I softened my stance and nodded before turning to Holden.

He and Beatrix were having a private conversation, but as soon as they saw me watching, she parted ways and disappeared without another word.

Holden strode my way, hands in his jean pockets. "Want to tell me what happened here?"

"I might have overreacted," I said.

"Care to elaborate so I have your side of the story instead of just Beatrix's?" Holden pressed.

"Not really."

He sighed. "This isn't going to work if you don't trust me, Foster."

Holden was right again, but trust was hard. Trust meant putting faith in someone else. It meant letting them in, which wasn't something I was used to any longer. But as I thought about Andie and what would be best for her, I knew there was more I needed to do, even if I didn't like it.

"When Andie said she was leaving, I let myself believe if I didn't go with her that she would get hurt without my protection, or worse, never come back. Then Beatrix began butting in and she once again tried to hurt me but ended up hurting Andie in the process."

That was something I wasn't sure I was going to forgive myself or the witch for anytime soon.

"You know I had a true mate, right?" Holden asked, and I nodded. "She died almost ten years ago now. We had almost eighty years together before she was taken from me. So much time has passed that I nearly forgot what it was like to fear losing the one meant just for you."

"What do you mean?" I asked, trying not to let myself panic when I felt Andie getting farther away.

She's going to be fine, my wolf reminded me.

She better be.

Holden continued. "When I met Annie, she was young and wild. Our wolves instantly connected like with any true mate bond amongst wolf shifters, but my Annie... She wasn't ready to settle down. She ran from me, and I gladly chased her. For weeks, that minx dodged me, but even though she was refusing me, I was getting to know her. Watching where she went, what she did, what she ate, and everything in between."

"How did you get her to stop running?" I asked, even though I didn't actually think Andie was running from me.

"I showed her I could be the man she was looking for. My Annie wanted a true partner to live life with, not someone to settle down with. I was older than her by nearly fifteen years, but I had no problem showing her that we had more in common than she realized. I think that's what you need to do here."

"I don't understand," I said.

Holden glanced behind me, a soft smile rising on his lips. "You've been through a lot, Foster. You've lost more than any man should have to lose in a lifetime. Those losses have changed you, but don't let them define you. I can already see how much you care for the girl, but from the sounds of it, she has a lot of growing to do, and this world isn't what she's used to."

"Are you telling me I need to let her go until she's adjusted?" I was suddenly regretting my choice to ask Holden for help and joining his pack.

"No, but I am saying that you need to take a step back. Look at the situation with fresh eyes. Andie isn't a wolf. She's a witch. That itself is your first problem, but now we also know that she's also a witch without her magic. Magic I assume that she needs to properly bond with you."

Shit. What irritated me most was that none of what Holden was saying was wrong. My wolf had already assumed the bit about Andie's magic, but knowing and accepting all of it wasn't an easy feat. Though, I'd do my best because that was what Andie deserved. My absolute best.

"Thank you, Holden. I'm glad you showed up when you did," I said earnestly.

"Me, too. Once they're back and we know what they found, then I can help you figure out how to proceed. Beatrix will back off, but you'll need to do so as well. It took me decades to get along with the witch, but you don't have that much time, and whether you want to believe this or not, she's worth having on your side."

I scoffed. I found that hard to believe after all I'd witnessed.

She did *try to help you when you first arrived,* my wolf said.

No, she tried to pawn me off on another pack.

Was she really trying to 'pawn you off'? Or was she doing

what's best for any wolf by giving you options for a place to call home? She might have gone about it the wrong way, but Beatrix was only giving you what she knew I needed.

My hands tightened into fists when I realized my wolf was speaking the truth. Maybe the witch wasn't as bad as I'd made her out to be.

Andie needs us all to get along. We can't make her choose once she's able to feel the bond. That wouldn't be fair to her, my wolf added.

Holden and my wolf were right, but getting a grip on my temper and the need to protect Andie wasn't easy. Not after everything I'd been through.

I glanced back toward where I knew the coven was and sucked in a breath. "They left."

Holden stood shoulder to shoulder with me. "We'll wait together."

"Thank you, Holden."

"You're one of mine now. No thanks necessary," he said.

The sincerity in his words had me relaxing slightly. I was grateful not to be waiting alone, but until I had Andie back in my sights, I wasn't going to be able to breathe right.

14

ANDIE

My head was swimming when Charlie practically carried me back within the coven's shield. My muscles twitched, and my brain wasn't communicating properly with my body to help me walk.

"The effects should wear off soon. I'm not an expert healer or you'd be better already," Charlie said when she stopped, waiting for Beatrix to slip back through the barrier.

I inhaled and exhaled slowly. My head was starting to pound, but something told me to look up instead of closing my eyes like I wanted to.

Foster's gaze was locked on me just like before. I didn't know how he did that, but I was beginning to like it more and more. As I stared back, his shoulders lost some of their tension and he nodded at me before turning away.

"If he wasn't so angry all the time, he'd be too hot for his own good," Charlie said.

"Something must have happened to him," I said. "He's not just angry. You can see it in his eyes. He's terrified of something."

"Huh. I missed that, but then again, I don't think I was supposed to see it."

I leaned over, bending my knees, and pressed my hands against my thighs. My head tilted forward, and a cascade of light-pink hair made a curtain around me when I finally closed my eyes.

"What did Beatrix do to me?" I asked, but it wasn't Charlie who answered.

"I was trying to stun the wolf. I might have had the voltage turned up a little higher than needed," Beatrix said dryly.

I slowly lifted my head back up, and she placed a hand over my chest where she'd got me with her magic. The spot warmed and my body straightened. Muscles in my arms and legs stopped twitching, and I had my energy back just as soon as she let go of me.

"I'm sorry, Andie," Beatrix said.

I nearly choked while I was brushing my hair back into place. "Thank you."

"I mean it. I'll even apologize to Foster when we're back. I don't want to make this harder on you. I let my desire to push people's buttons go too far. You shouldn't have gotten hurt in the process," she added.

"That means a lot to me, and I think it will to Foster as well," I replied.

She grunted. "I'm not sure he'll accept, but I'll follow through. Now, let's get going. The portal is ready to be opened."

She hurried ahead. For an older witch, she moved quickly, and I had to lengthen my stride to keep up with her swift steps.

When we arrived back in the courtyard, Benjamin and

Ava were standing a few feet apart with Evelyn in front of them.

Evelyn glanced back. "We don't have all day."

"What are you waiting for then?" Beatrix retorted. She was back to the snarkiness that I'd been witnessing since my return.

Evelyn glared, but she didn't say anything else before rubbing her palms together. Ava and Benjamin held their arms out with one hand facing each other and the other toward Evelyn.

When Evelyn pulled her palms apart, silver magic extended out of her hands and connected with Ava's and Benjamin's. She walked closer to them, bringing one of her arms up and the other down. I watched carefully, then jumped back when the position of her hands switched, and a loud bang sounded.

Ava and Benjamin moved toward Evelyn while a small circle began swirling in front of them, doubling in size with each second that passed until it was six feet in diameter.

"Let's go," Beatrix said, grabbing my hand.

I glanced back to make sure Charlie was coming, but she was already at my side, looping her arm through mine. "Together. Just like I said."

I smiled and brought my attention forward. The portal had metallic liquid moving around the exterior, and on the other side was the back door to my house in Montana. Holy hell, they'd actually done it.

I wasn't sure why I was so surprised when I'd already been teleported from Montana to here, but still, this was weird.

We walked quickly through, and Ava stayed in the courtyard when Benjamin turned to close the opening.

"Why are they closing it?" I asked Charlie.

"We don't want anyone sneaking into our coven while we're busy, and the longer it's open, the higher the risk of us being noticed by other witches," she answered.

"Hurry," Beatrix barked, effectively ending our conversation.

The old witch rushed to my back porch and instead of asking me for a key, she blasted through the door with magic, turning the wood into shards.

"Get the necklace," she demanded, but I was frozen in place when I glanced around my home.

The picture frames that hung on my wall were lying broken on the carpet. My cupboards had been ripped open, the contents now smashed onto the tile and counters.

"Come on, Andie. We've got this," Charlie whispered into my ear before she urged me along.

I tried to avert my eyes from seeing any other damage, but my bedroom was more of the same. My mattress had been blown to bits. Feathers from my down comforter covered half the room.

"Where's the necklace?" Charlie asked, doing her best to keep me on track.

"The closet." I pointed and moved in that direction, but she beat me to it.

When she slid open the door on the side I gestured to, I was crushed.

The jewelry box was there, but it was smashed into tiny pieces. I bent to the ground, sorting through the mess, but the necklace was nowhere to be seen.

"It's not here," I muttered. My eyes and throat burned as I tried to process the situation. "It's not here," I repeated, louder.

"It's going to be okay, Andie," Charlie said softly.

"Is it? Because I can't see how that's possible right now. Everything in my house is ruined. The landlord is probably going to sue me for the damages because I can't afford to repair all of this. Nothing about any of this is *okay*," I snapped, doing my best to focus on the anger inside me so that I didn't break down in tears like I really wanted.

Charlie helped me stand, pulling me into her arms. "We're going to fix this together. I know everything feels broken right now, but remember you're not alone, Andie. We'll help you, but right now, we need to go."

The moment she mentioned leaving, the air around me became heavy, like when we'd been attacked in the street. Breathing was near impossible, my chest ached, and the tingles along my arms were coming back.

"Incoming!" Evelyn shouted from the living room.

Charlie grabbed my arm, pulling me down the hallway. "Run, Andie. You have to get out of here!" She shoved me toward Benjamin, who was standing behind Evelyn and caught me with ease. He started pulling me toward the back door when the front one was kicked in.

"Hello, Beatrix," a woman's maniacal voice cooed over the chaos.

Benjamin tugged harder on me, but I dug my feet into the carpet and watched Charlie and Beatrix prepare for a fight. Charlie held a glowing yellow orb in each of her hands while Beatrix had sparks of silver flickering around her.

"Give me the necklace, Ruby," Beatrix demanded.

Ruby glanced at me while I fought Benjamin, who was trying to pull me out the back door. Her sage eyes bored into my soul, and she flicked her chocolate-colored hair back with a smirk. "Give me the girl."

"Over my dead body," Beatrix replied, sending a wave of her silver magic at the newcomer.

"I think I can make that happen." Ruby dodged the first blast of Beatrix's energy and didn't hesitate to retaliate. Her dark-grey, almost-black magic collided with Beatrix's, and Charlie moved to join in. Before I could see what happened next, Benjamin forcefully tossed me over his shoulder.

"Sorry, Andie, but we gotta go," he said, moving out the back door.

"What if there are more attackers and Charlie and Beatrix need help?" I asked.

"Then I'll come back, but my job is to first keep you safe. Back to the coven you go." He set me down and stepped next to Evelyn. They pressed their hands together, presumably to open the portal again.

While they were occupied, I considered running back inside, especially when I heard loud grunts and too many bangs to be good for anyone, but I had to be smart. No matter how much I wanted to make sure they were safe, I knew I'd only be a distraction.

"Is there anything—" I began to ask, but my words were cut off when something scorching slammed between my shoulder blades.

I lurched forward, landing hard on my hands and knees. Benjamin and Evelyn were still locked together by their hands and had their eyes closed, meaning I was on my own for the moment.

As I tried to stand, someone grabbed on to my hair, lifting me up before pinning my arms to my sides. "Your friend isn't going to save you this time."

The man who had attacked me the night before spun me toward him and grinned, showing off perfectly straight yet yellowing teeth that I hadn't noticed during our previous meeting.

His midnight eyes sparked with glee and his hands warmed over my skin. "You're coming with me."

If he teleported with me, I was dead. I knew it. Still, I might not have had magic, but I hadn't been defenseless against this asshole last night and I wasn't going to be this time, either.

My head slammed into his. Bones cracked, and I hissed in pain. My eyes pinched closed before I forced them back open again.

My hit loosened the guy's hold on me, then I kneed him in the balls, bringing him to his knees.

"I'm not going anywhere with you," I sneered, then ran for the portal that was just beginning to open.

Except Benjamin and Evelyn closed it as soon as they saw I wasn't alone anymore.

I continued to run toward them, but the warlock I'd just injured had already recovered from my hit. He sent out a stream of energy that wrapped around my ankle, and I fell toward the ground. Thankfully, Benjamin caught me before I faceplanted.

"I got you," he said with bright eyes before yanking hard on my arms and blasting at the dark magic at my feet.

I cried out, not only from my bones being pulled out of sockets, but because of the burning sensation growing between my shoulder blades. What had been numb moments before was coming to life by the second.

"It burns," I murmured against Benjamin's chest when he pulled me farther away from where Evelyn was fighting against the other witch.

"Hang in there," he said.

Considering he was probably a teenager from the looks of his boyish face, I was impressed with how calm he was staying. His hands were steady, holding me gently while quickly getting me to the opposite side of the yard.

"We need to get out of here, but I'm not supposed to teleport back to the coven," he said once we'd stopped moving.

"We can't leave the others," I begged. Evelyn was fighting the warlock who had attacked me, but he didn't seem to be tiring. If we had any chance of opening the secure portal, that asshole needed to be dead sooner rather than later.

"Go help her. I'll be fine here," I said, pathetically trying to push him away.

"Beatrix would kill me if she knew I left your side."

"Then it can be our secret."

Benjamin took another look back before nodding at me. "Two minutes. If he's not dead before then, we leave no matter what."

"Clock's ticking. Go on," I said.

As soon as Benjamin darted away, I started to fall toward the ground. Whatever was going on with my back wasn't good. The smart thing to do would have been to let Benjamin teleport me, but these other witches had been waiting for us. I couldn't stand the thought of Charlie, Beatrix, Evelyn, or Benjamin getting hurt, or worse, because of me.

Once I was resting on my side, I focused on the fight between the three witches and sighed in relief when Benjamin created a shield-like orb between his hands. He quickly shoved the light energy forward and it knocked the other warlock to the ground.

Evelyn jumped on top of him, pressing her hands over his chest. I heard her grunt even from where I was lying, and then smoke began to rise around her.

Benjamin backed up a step, coughing as he did so, then he ran back to me. He dropped to his knees next to me, gently lifting me up. "That was almost too easy, which isn't good. We're going to get out of here now."

"What about Charlie and Beatrix?" I asked weakly.

"They'll be right behind us."

I couldn't hear anything from inside, which I hoped *was* a good thing. Even so, that Ruby witch they'd been fighting hadn't looked like an amateur, so there would be no comfort until I saw Beatrix and Charlie for myself.

"Hurry up. More are coming," Evelyn called to us.

She was on her feet again, and the guy attacking us was nowhere to be seen.

"What happened to him?" I asked Benjamin.

"She disintegrated him once I helped with the distraction," he answered, like that was a normal, everyday action.

I wanted to ask a million questions about how the hell that was even possible, but Charlie and Beatrix were hobbling out of the house together. It was time to go.

Benjamin steadied me. "Can you stand?"

I nodded, and he went to Evelyn. Their palms pressed together, but this time, Charlie joined them, and the portal was opened in half the time.

Ava stood on the other side with narrow eyes, glaring at me.

Charlie stumbled into me before I could ask what Ava's problem was. Both of us began to sway, but Benjamin was right there, happily holding on to us.

"Come on, ladies. Let's get you both fixed up."

We were back in the courtyard and the portal was closed, but my chest tightened. Something still wasn't right.

"Someone needs to shut that wolf up before one of our members does so in their own way," Ava barked, helping Evelyn with a wound on her arm.

"What's wrong with Foster?" I asked, gripping Benjamin's forearm.

Ava looked me up and down. "You."

15

FOSTER

The five minutes that Beatrix had said they'd be gone was nearly up. My unease grew with every step I paced along the road, then doubled when a chill ran through me. A chill wouldn't necessarily have been out of the ordinary, except there wasn't even a slight breeze blowing over us.

I stopped mid-stride and listened for anything that didn't belong, but all my ears found were the sounds of birds chirping and small animals skittering along the forest floor behind us.

Holden grabbed my forearm. "What's wrong?"

"I don't know, but something isn't right." I stepped toward the barrier, but he jerked me back.

"You don't want to find out the hard way what happens to supernaturals who touch Beatrix's shield," Holden warned.

I snarled in return. I'd told myself I was going to be nicer to the witch, but as the agitation inside me grew, I was finding that promise hard to keep.

"We have to get inside or at least get someone to come tell us what's going on," I said.

"How do you know anything is happening?" Holden asked.

My hand covered my chest. "I just know."

He nodded. "We can't see or hear them, but they should be able to see and hear us."

I backed up several paces and shifted without telling Holden what I was doing.

She's going to be okay, my wolf said, shaking out his fur.

I didn't bother to respond to his optimism. Instead, I urged him to howl. Loudly.

My wolf did as requested, and Holden backed up even farther, covering his ears.

"You're going to piss them off," he said once the second howl was cut off.

That's what I'm hoping for, I said through my newly formed connection to the alpha.

Holden shook his head at me, and my wolf kept howling. I had no idea how long it would take the witches to come, but I wasn't going to stop until they did.

After about our tenth sound-off, the barrier shimmered. A warlock stepped out, glaring first at me, then at Holden. His eyes were a dark jade, and his russet hair was shaved short. He wore black pants with a loose three-button white shirt and had a dagger strapped to each of his hips.

"*What* is your problem, Wolf?" he demanded.

I shifted back to two feet, so Holden didn't have to speak for me. "Is Beatrix back?"

"No. The portal opened but then closed. Why?"

I snarled at him, then curled my hands into fists and took a step forward. "Let me inside."

He laughed. "That's not happening."

I took another step and so did Holden. "Easy, Foster. You need them more than they need you."

"My mate is with Beatrix. You need to let me in so I can help them," I said, trying and failing to keep the sneer off my face.

"I can't do that. You're going to have to wait until Beatrix is back," he said.

"And if she doesn't come back?" I spat. "If they all die because they didn't have enough help, their blood will be on *your* hands, and I'll rip you to shreds for denying me."

He scoffed at me. "Threaten me one more time and see if you ever step foot in this coven again."

"He didn't mean to threaten you," Holden said as he held me back. "Let them know we're waiting when they're back, please."

The warlock disappeared back behind the barrier, and I roared. "Why would you let him go?"

"I've been leading for a long time, Foster. One thing I've learned is that I rarely get what I want when I *demand* it. You have to treat other supernaturals just like you would your own pack. More importantly, you must learn to work with them. I've been trying to teach you the same thing when it comes to Beatrix, and that notion applies to all of her coven."

I kicked the gravel in front of me and turned away. I knew Holden was right. I'd been an alpha myself for five years, but being nice had only gotten my pack killed. Whatever diplomatic skills I'd had in me before, those were dead. Along with the rest of my pack.

I only cared about one thing and that was making sure Andie was okay.

Though, as the knot in my chest expanded, my hope that everything would be fine continued to shrink.

16

ANDIE

The burn in my shoulders was growing more intense by the second. As much as I wanted to figure out what was going on with Foster, I wasn't sure I could stand for much longer.

Benjamin let go of Charlie and picked me up, cradling me against his chest. "Andie needs a healer."

"Charlie's hurt worse," I muttered when his arm pressed against my scorching skin.

He adjusted his hold lower and he eyed Beatrix. "You and Charlie are in no shape to help, and Andie's going to need someone experienced since she doesn't have her own magic to speed up the process."

"You didn't get the necklace?" Ava cut in.

Beatrix pinched the bridge of her nose. "No. Moira's witches had already gone through the house before we got there, and a few were waiting for us when we showed up." Beatrix paused, then looked over at me and Benjamin. "Take her to Charlie's. I'll send someone over."

"What about Foster?" I asked when a howl echoed through the air around us.

Beatrix's lips thinned. "Ava, please let Foster in and tell him she's at Charlie's. Given he went there last night instead of leaving like I told him to, he should know where to go."

Apparently, nothing got past the coven leader, but I wasn't going to apologize for asking Foster to stay longer.

"Are you sure, Bea? I sent Chase out to shut the wolf up earlier and he wasn't very nice," Ava said.

Beatrix sighed. "It will be better for Andie to have him close."

Ava's lip curled. "He's really her soulmate?"

"So it seems."

Benjamin turned me toward Charlie, stopping me from snapping at the witches for talking as if I wasn't present.

"Can you walk, or should I come back for you?" he asked Charlie.

She kneeled against one of the concrete benches. "I'm fine. I'll go with Beatrix to make sure the healer is quick for Andie."

"Are you sure?" I asked her. She had blood seeping from her hairline and a bubbling wound on the arm that was holding one side of her ribs.

She nodded. "I look worse than I am."

Benjamin secured his hold around me and began walking away. I focused on him instead of the fire that seemed to be blistering my back with each step taken.

His face was smooth, and there were more freckles on his pale skin than I'd noticed before. He didn't even have facial hair, just peach fuzz.

"How old are you?" I asked.

"Seventeen."

Hmm, he must have been a late bloomer or things like puberty were different for witches and warlocks. Given we aged so much slower than humans, I assumed it was the latter.

"Charlie said you didn't really leave your house much before Beatrix asked for your help. Why was that?" I asked. I wanted to stay distracted until whatever healer showed up. Fighting back tears was getting harder by the second.

He shrugged. "When Beatrix told me your story, I knew I couldn't say *no*."

"Charlie mentioned you're a tracker?" I pressed, wanting to know more.

Benjamin nodded but didn't respond with words.

"And that's a skill you got from your father?" I asked.

He chuckled. "You're not going to let this go, are you?"

I winced and gasped louder than I'd meant to from his movements, then smirked. "Not likely. I need something to distract me, and your hesitation to answer my questions tells me you have an interesting story to tell."

"You're lucky that you're hurt and that I feel bad since I was in charge of getting you out of there. I'm not supposed to tell other people this, but since you're special like me, I guess it can't hurt. My parents were trackers for Moira. She held them captive until my mom got pregnant with me. My mom and dad hatched a plan to escape together, but only my mom made it out."

My heart hurt for Benjamin. I knew what it was like to be raised without a father, given, until recently, I couldn't remember him ever being around.

"Beatrix found us after I was born and offered to let us join her, but my mom declined at first. She no longer had a desire to live within a coven, but it wasn't long after that my magic started to increase, and my mom knew she needed more help to keep me safe."

"How did your mom know when you were so young?" I asked.

"Well, I guess I started to glow a few weeks after I was born, and I wouldn't stop until Beatrix came back. She put a shield around me that faded over time while I learned to gain control over my magic. Since then, I've worked to make the father I never knew proud and have become an expert tracker, but your aunt was smarter than even Beatrix thought. Whatever spell the two of you wove was more complicated than any I've ever seen."

Aunt Junie. More than anything, I wished I could talk to her. As much as I missed my mother, I knew my aunt wouldn't have held anything back from me. If only I'd searched for her when I'd had the chance instead of hoping she'd just pop up again one day. That was a choice that would haunt me for a long time.

"Thank you for trying to help. Not many kids your age would do that," I said, remembering when I'd been seventeen and had wanted nothing to do with responsibility.

Benjamin opened the door to Charlie's house and frowned. "Hey, I'm not a kid."

I laughed, then regretted the action as I groaned. "Sure, you're not, peach fuzz."

"Andie!" Foster's voice roared from the path behind us.

Benjamin turned around with me still in his arms, and the poor kid's eyes went wide when Foster's imposing form was storming quickly toward us.

"You can set me down, Benjamin," I said. "Thank you for all of your help and for sharing part of your story."

He slowly put me on my feet, then gulped. "Uh, I was going to wait for the healer with you."

"Probably best if you didn't," I replied.

Foster snarled at Benjamin, and I snapped my fingers at the wolf shifter. "Leave him alone or we're going to have serious problems."

Foster jerked back at my words, and I continued.

"Benjamin was only helping me back to the house while Charlie found me a healer." I nodded at Benjamin. "Thank you again for everything you did."

He was inching out the door, trying to give Foster a wide berth. "Yeah. No problem."

I glared at Foster, making sure he didn't scare Benjamin any further, then grabbed on to the couch when my legs grew too shaky to stand on. My back turned as I did so, giving Foster his first look at the injury I had no desire to see.

His chest rumbled louder than I'd yet to hear. "Who hurt you?"

"A witch that the teenager you were just terrorizing helped kill," I replied, trying to make my way to the couch so I could lie on my stomach. Tears filled my eyes from the pain I could no longer ignore.

Foster grabbed my hand to help, but I jerked it away from him. "Listen, I might not understand what you're feeling right now, but I also know that no matter how strong of a pull you have toward me, it doesn't give you the right to be a jerk to everyone else. I understand not getting along with Beatrix, but I won't put up with you going all caveman on anyone who's near me. You need to get your shit together, Foster."

My increased pain levels were making me emotional *and*

cranky, but that didn't make my words any less true. While I normally wouldn't have been so blunt, I'd said what I'd said and wasn't sorry for it.

Foster froze where he was, and I crawled over the arm of the couch, using my arms to pull myself along until I could lie down without bending my back awkwardly.

As soon as I closed my eyes and sighed, I sensed Foster staring at me. I cracked one of mine open to find him kneeling on the ground beside me.

"I'm sorry," he whispered.

"For what?" I asked. I needed to know he truly understood the problem.

"For losing control. I'm not always like this. Or at least, I didn't used to be. I don't want you to think I'm some possessive psycho who doesn't care about what you want when that's the complete opposite of how I think."

"Just remember that actions speak louder than words," I replied softly, once again losing myself in his cobalt stare. There was so much hurt there that I wanted to unravel, even though I didn't know him at all.

I tried and failed to fight my softening heart when he reached a hand up, stroking my forearm.

"What can I do for you?" he asked.

"Tell me a story while we wait for Charlie and the healer," I said. I didn't want to get into anything heavy when I felt like welcoming death to my door.

Foster tensed and I reclosed my eyes, hoping that would help him feel more comfortable. Also, partly because exhaustion was trying to smother me.

I felt him adjust his position, and I smiled when he covered my one exposed hand with his, then cleared his throat.

"A long time ago, I lived in a wolf pack about an hour outside of Fairbanks, Alaska. We didn't have a lot of wolves, but we were family and everything about our home made me feel safe. During the winter months, I'd hide from my parents, wanting to sleep outside even when the snow was two-to three-feet deep. Watching the Northern Lights dance across the sky with their varying shades of green, blue, and magenta was the best part of my day. I was the only child in the pack who hated the long summer days."

He paused, and I squeezed his hand as encouragement to keep going.

"There was a boreal owl that would join me regardless of whether I was in my human or wolf form. He would fly over me while I raced through the thick forest, searching for clear skies to watch the colorful sky. Sometimes I'd run for miles, because the farther away I went, the longer it took my parents to drag me back home. It wasn't until I was a teenager that they stopped coming after me."

"How long would you stay out there?" I murmured, my eyes still shut.

His thumb stroked over my palm, making goosebumps rise along my arms.

"A week was the longest my mother could stand, and my father would come get me," Foster replied, and I could hear the smile in his words.

I peeked at him, wanting to see for myself, and sucked in a breath at seeing him with his walls down. His deep blue gaze was lighter than I'd yet to see and, while he stared at our joined hands, the creases between his brows faded away, revealing a calm Foster I hoped to see more of.

"Why did you leave Alaska if you loved it so much?" I asked, and he caught me staring.

I expected him to close off from me, but his expression became pained and his grip on me tightened. "I didn't do so by choice."

When he didn't elaborate, I wanted to push for more, but Charlie came bursting through the door. "Andie?"

"On the couch," I called back, holding on to Foster so he didn't feel like he had to go now that she was home.

"I have Camille with me. She's going to fix you right up," Charlie said before she came into my view. Her head no longer had fresh blood coating her blonde strands, and the bubbling wound I'd seen on her arm was nothing more than a faint pink scar. A relief that she really was okay swept through me.

Camille appeared behind Charlie. She avoided eye contact and flinched when she caught sight of Foster next to me. She brushed a strand of short, brunette hair behind her ear and lifted her chocolate eyes. "We'll need to take your shirt off," she said softly.

"Do you want me to leave?" Foster asked me.

I might have asked him to go if he hadn't offered, but I could see he was learning lessons with each of our interactions. I didn't want to push him away, as long as he could stop being so overbearing.

I shook my head. "Stay and help."

Foster lifted me up by my hips, and Charlie came around the front when I rested on my elbows.

"I'm going to tear the shirt while he's holding you. There's a really good possibility that it's burned into your skin, so maybe bite down on that pillow," Charlie said.

Foster kept my middle elevated while I put more pressure on my shaking arms. I really didn't want to scream in front of all of them, but I also wasn't fond of tearing into a pillow with my teeth like a savage.

"I was trying to say it nicely, but I need you to take me seriously, Andie. Bite the damn pillow," Charlie added as politely as she could.

With a heavy sigh, I grabbed the throw pillow, and just as I brought the linen material close to my face, Charlie gave my shirt a swift tug.

"Mother fucking fucker!" I screeched, and hot tears swam in my eyes until I buried my face in the pillow.

"I'm so sorry, Andie. One more time. That was only one side," Charlie said.

"Can't one of you dull the pain?" Foster asked with a cracked voice. His grip tightened around my hips where he was still holding me.

"Not with the dark magic growing inside her," Camille replied softly. "It will only make my job harder."

I braced myself for Charlie's next move, wanting to get this over with, and shoved the pillow into my mouth. This time when I screamed, there were no obscenities, but instead, I tore the fabric between my teeth and tasted bland cotton fibers in the next second.

I bucked involuntarily when my pain levels spiked, and Foster's thumbs stroked over my newly exposed skin. "We're going to set you back down, Andie," he murmured, and I nodded.

My chin trembled, and I swallowed hard, turning my head so I could see them once I was lying back down on my stomach, sans my borrowed shirt.

Charlie had backed up, and Foster moved closer to my face. He wiped my tears away before cupping my cheek but said nothing when I tried to focus on him instead of the agony storming through me.

That failed a second later when I flinched and bit my lip thanks to the cool hands that began poking around my back.

"Sorry. I should have warned you that I was going to start. Do you want to know what I'm doing?" Camille asked.

"Not a fucking chance." I groaned. A play-by-play was the last thing I needed while I was dying on the couch.

My eyes continued to water, and Foster stayed within my view.

"Everything is going to be fine, Andie," he murmured, wiping more of my newly shed tears from my cheeks.

I sure as hell hoped so, because while Camille pressed her freezing hands over my barbequed skin, I was oh-so-tempted to reach back and claw her eyes out.

Instead, I gripped Foster's hand and gritted my teeth, keeping my murderous thoughts to myself.

17

FOSTER

Seeing Andie with the burns on her back gutted me. I wanted to lash out, but Holden's earlier advice echoed in my mind. I needed the coven and, as much as that pissed me off, I had to learn how to use that knowledge to my benefit instead of letting it be a problem.

I tossed around thoughts about how I could do that while I watched Camille work on Andie. My mate had been hit with a stream of dark magic. The center between her shoulder blades had a third-degree burn about six inches in diameter, and the inky energy had spread, leaving thin lines of black that fanned out like a spiderweb all the way up to her neck.

Andie's grip on my hand tightened when her body tensed, and I made the mistake of looking again at the wounds.

Camille was peeling fried skin from Andie's back. I wanted to rage at the sight, but Andie needed me to be calm for her, so that was what I was.

"She's almost done," I said to Andie, brushing hair from her ashen face.

Charlie cocked her head at me from behind the couch when she heard my lie. It was more of a stretch of the truth, and it was what Andie needed to hear.

As soon as Andie did, she let out a heavy sigh and closed her eyes again. Hopefully, she'd pass out from the pain and miss the worst of what was going on.

"What happened?" I asked Charlie when Andie's tension lessened.

"Nearly worst-case scenario. The house had already been trashed, the necklace we needed to get back was gone, and some of Moira's witches were still waiting for us. Evelyn said Andie was waiting for the portal to be reopened when she got hit."

I did my best to stay calm. Reminding them that I should have been there to help wasn't going to change anything now.

"This energy that hit her, it's darker than anything I've ever seen before," Camille added.

"How so?" I asked.

She pointed to the black lines along Andie's back. "That isn't natural, even by magical standards. And the foreign magic is fighting being removed, almost like it's trying to attach itself to what little born-magic Andie does have inside her. I can get everything that doesn't belong out, but without her magical assistance, it's going to take hours more."

Andie groaned. "That's not what I wanted to hear."

I'd hoped she was mostly unconscious, but apparently, I'd been wrong.

"At least you're not stuck with the dark magic until we get your necklace back," Charlie said.

"What does the necklace have to do with this?" I asked.

Charlie leaned against the wall, still facing me. "Well, Beatrix already told you that Andie doesn't have all of her magic, but what she didn't tell you was that we originally thought Andie's aunt had concealed the energy. We were wrong. The magic was placed in a necklace since Andie wasn't old enough to willingly give her consent for a complete removal. With the necklace taken, she won't be able to properly use her magic or understand who she is."

She likely won't properly feel the bond until she has the rest back, my wolf said, but I'd already come to the same conclusion.

At least she's not pushing us away. She feels *something*, I added.

Instead of being angry that things hadn't gone as expected, I reminded myself that things could have been worse. Much worse. Andie could have flat-out rejected us.

"How do we get the necklace back now?" I watched Andie's face for any other signs that she was still in pain, but Camille was being gentle, which I appreciated.

"We'll need to talk to Beatrix," Charlie answered. "Moira has a coven hidden deep in Louisiana. She draws part of her dark energy from New Orleans, where idiot humans like to do stupid shit in hopes that they'll unlock some magical power inside themselves that doesn't exist. Her shield is just as powerful as Beatrix's, and their coven won't be easy to locate."

Not being easy didn't mean *impossible* and I was going to figure this out. Not only for the bond I wanted Andie to feel, but so she'd be capable of protecting herself. What had happened to her wasn't acceptable, and my mate deserved to feel whole.

"There's more you need to know," Charlie said softly, peeking at Andie, whose face was slack.

I nodded for her to continue.

"I'm not sure how much you know about our kind, but Andie isn't just part of one of our founding lines, she's the last living member of one. Her dad and aunt had been the only other living members for some time. With them gone, Moira is desperate to get her hands on Andie and tap into that family line, and she just might be able to with that necklace now in her possession."

My ire skyrocketed, but instead of unleashing my fury, I took a calming breath, bottling the feeling up for later, and stared at Andie's resting face. In that moment, I made a silent vow that wouldn't be broken.

I vowed to do whatever it took to get Andie's magic back. To make sure that dark witch never got her hands on my mate. To kill any who thought they could come for what was mine.

That *witch* would soon regret the day she came after my mate. I would rip the world apart before I let anyone hurt Andie again.

———

THE SUN HAD ALREADY SET BY THE TIME ANDIE WOKE BACK UP. Camille had finished withdrawing the dark magic a couple of hours prior and thought Andie would be out the rest of the evening, but I stayed anyway and was glad I had.

"Hey," I said when Andie began to stir.

She squinted and scrunched her face. "Where am I?"

"Charlie's bedroom."

She groaned, trying to sit up, and I moved to help her.

She didn't flinch when I touched her ribs, so I took that to mean she really was feeling better.

"Why is it so dark?" she asked once she was leaning against the headboard.

"Because you've been passed out all day. What do you need?" I asked.

She closed her eyes and stretched her neck a few times before reopening them. "I don't know. Where's Charlie?"

"She's with the group you went with earlier. She'll be back soon."

Charlie had been standing watch most of the day with me, but I'd finally sent her away when she wouldn't stop pacing. I'd known she'd also wanted to see what Beatrix was up to, and I was capable of looking after Andie.

"I'm surprised you're still here," Andie said with a crooked grin.

I returned the gesture. "They couldn't have kicked me out if they'd tried."

She grimaced. "Did they? Try, that is?"

I gave Andie's hand a squeeze. "No, but I haven't left the house since I entered the coven. Though, I don't intend to give Beatrix a reason to ask me to leave. Not anymore."

I had done a lot of thinking and talking with my wolf while I'd sat beside the bed, waiting for Andie to wake up. As I'd already known deep down and been reminded of by Holden, I needed to treat this situation as I would have a business deal when I'd been an alpha.

Well, except for when it came to interacting with Andie.

First, I needed the witches to trust me. I knew Andie was still going to need time, and I wanted to be around as much as she would have me. I couldn't do that if I was so damn furious with everyone all the time.

"Can you help me up?" she asked.

I was on my feet before she even finished speaking. She took both of my hands, and her arms were shaking. "Maybe you should stay in bed a while longer," I suggested.

Her rosy cheeks turned a brighter pink. "I need to use the bathroom."

I bent forward. "Put your arm over my shoulder."

Andie's fingers slid across the back of my neck, and I tensed when her warmth soaked into me. Lifting her up, I took a deep inhale but regretted the action when her sweet scent of roses and sage hit me in the center of my chest.

"Are you okay?" she asked hesitantly.

I nodded, afraid to speak while I carried her to the bathroom.

I nudged the door open with my boot and slowly set Andie down in front of the sink and closest to the toilet. She looked up at me with innocent eyes. "Thank you."

"Call for me when you're done," I said, then I closed the door behind me before I walked to the kitchen. I didn't think she'd appreciate me standing there listening to her take care of business.

I made myself at home and opened the fridge. My warming opinion of Charlie increased when I saw several beers sitting on the shelf. I reached for one and popped the top open, leaning against the counter.

The cool liquid bubbled, but I didn't wait for the head to fizz out before I took a long pull. The taste was sour and fruity all at the same time. Not my kind of beer, but I finished the bottle in a few drinks anyway, needing the distraction.

When I was done, I stepped into the hallway and found

Andie hobbling out of the bedroom. I went to her, reaching my hands out in case she needed more help.

"I need to walk. I've been in bed too long," she said.

I stayed with her just in case she got tired too quickly, but I kept my hands to myself. She circled the dining room table before entering the living room and eyeing the couch.

"Do you want to sit?" I asked.

She shook her head. "I was remembering being mad at you, then how much I appreciated you not leaving me when Charlie and Camille showed up."

"I'm sorry for how I acted with Benjamin," I said, because I couldn't remember if I'd actually apologized before.

"It's not me you need to say sorry to, but I appreciate the sentiment." She paused, resting against the arm of the couch, then looked up at me with hooded eyes. "I don't know what this is between us."

"What do you mean?" I asked, and my breathing increased while sweat built on my neck. I wasn't ever nervous, but the thought of finally talking with Andie about the bond between us made my mouth dry.

"Maybe I should sit down now." Andie turned for the couch and I helped her before sitting as well, making sure to give her some space, even though my hands itched to caress her creamy skin.

"Better?" I asked.

She leaned her head back and nodded. "Can you tell me about the bond? What does it feel like to you?"

I brushed a shaky hand through my hair and looked anywhere but at Andie. I wasn't much for talking about my feelings. I never had been. But I also knew Andie needed this more than I did.

"When most wolves find their mates, they don't know who they are until they see them. It was different for me. Months ago, the creator of wolf shifters called the Moon Goddess appeared in my mind. She told me that you were out there somewhere, but she didn't say who you were or even what you were. She only gifted me with your scent."

"What do I smell like?" Andie asked with a light laugh.

I grinned. "Roses and sage. I think the sage comes from your family magic, because that's what I smelled most when I first arrived in L.A."

"I don't understand why my scent led you here instead of to where I was," she said.

"I've thought about that, too, and I'd have to ask Beatrix to know for sure, but I think your magic scent was shared with your aunt. Given she was actively practicing when I arrived, it was her who drew me here, but it was my wolf who believed you'd eventually show up even as the scent began to fade. He has a lot more patience than I do."

"He's a lot bigger than I expected. Though, I'm a little embarrassed to admit I thought he was a dog at first."

I should be insulted by that, but I'm choosing not to be, my wolf said, and I chuckled.

"What?" Andie asked.

"My wolf. He's used to being intimidating, not compared to a house pet."

Her eyes widened. "You can talk to him?"

I nodded. "He's been in my head for as long as I can remember."

"I bet that's nice."

I shrugged. "It has its pros and cons."

I'll show you some of the cons if you want to keep complaining, my wolf added.

Easy, boy. We're just getting her talking.

"What happened when you saw me?" she asked.

As much as I wasn't sure how to put into words the feelings the mere sight of Andie had invoked inside me, I couldn't deny her request. Not when she looked at me with such clear longing and a need for understanding.

"When I saw you step outside the barrier, the first thing I felt was relief that we'd finally found you. After that was purpose. I knew that no matter what came next, making sure you were happy, safe, and healthy would always come before all else. I was able to let go of fears I've been holding on to for years in exchange for allowing the bond inside me to grow. The desire to know who you are, what would make you smile or frown and everything in between, was so palpable that my chest ached from anticipation. Most importantly, I knew then that you were mine. The other half of my soul."

Andie's eyes never broke from mine while I spoke. Not even when they welled with tears.

I reached for her hand. "I'm sorry. I shouldn't have said all of that."

She shook her head. "That was the most beautiful and honest thing I've ever heard anyone say. I'm not crying because I'm upset or scared. I'm jealous that I didn't get the chance to experience the same thing."

I slid closer to her, the need to hold her too strong to ignore any longer. "One day soon, I hope you will. We'll find your necklace and you'll get the magic you're supposed to have, which I believe will be the key to you feeling the bond."

She nestled her head against my chest and sighed. "Even

though there hasn't been an 'aha' moment for me, there's still something there. I hope you know that."

I pressed my lips to the top of her head. "Thank you."

Hearing her say those words had my chest swelling and skin warming. My fingers brushed through her pale-pink hair before gliding down her arm and circling around her tattoo, which I hadn't gotten a good look at until getting her into the bed earlier.

A black feather started underneath her bicep and the tip curled around the top of her arm with a dozen or more birds soaring out and away from the feather's point.

"Does this have a meaning for you?" I asked.

She glanced down at the tattoo. "My mom loved birdwatching on the beach. After she passed, I got this in her honor."

"Tell me about her."

Andie's smile grew, and she burrowed further into me. I tightened my hold around her and held in the sigh of satisfaction I wanted to let out while she began telling me stories of her childhood.

Bond or not, I had Andie in my arms. That would be enough for now.

18

———

ANDIE

Time passed without me even realizing. I told Foster dozens of stories from my childhood and the last few years while I'd navigated life without my mother. He listened intently, making me feel like he truly cared about every word spoken and wasn't just indulging me.

I'd had enough talking about me and wanted to know more about why he carried so much hurt inside him, though.

"I can tell you don't like talking about it, but can you tell me what happened to your old pack?" I asked.

His eyes darkened and jaw tensed as he turned away from me.

"I'm sorry. You don't have to," I said quietly.

Foster shook his head. "It's not that I don't want to tell you. I just don't want you to think less of me once I do."

I reached for his arm. "Unless you murdered a bunch of people, I don't think that could be a problem."

I was trying to lighten the mood, but he only seemed to glower more. "Then I guess we have a problem."

My instinct was to pull back from him, but I had a feeling he wasn't portraying the story accurately. "How about you let me decide if that's the case after you explain?"

Foster turned back to me and grabbed both of my hands. He was trembling, and I hated that whatever had happened so many years ago still plagued him this much.

"The pack I was raised in, the one I was telling you about in Alaska… I became the alpha of that pack after the other was ready to move on to warmer parts of the world with less responsibility. For five years, I ran the pack the same as he always had. We thrived, even in the winter months, and our people were happy. Something that wasn't always easy to accomplish in the middle of nowhere."

He paused and I squeezed his hand. "It sounds like they were lucky to have you."

"No, they weren't. I killed them all."

Now I really knew he was telling the story wrong. There was no way he'd killed his entire pack, but I didn't try to correct him. I waited for him to find his own words.

"A little over ten years ago, two brothers were passing through our area. They wanted to find a new pack and were tired of the city life. They were about my age at the time, which was thirty-five. They knew a lot about fishing and hunting and all the things we enjoyed most out in the Alaskan wilderness. So when they asked to stay, I said *yes*. Only they weren't the shifters they'd said they were."

My heart was already breaking on Foster's behalf. I could see where the story was going and wanted to stop him, save him from the pain of reliving the past, but I also knew the only way for him to move forward was to talk about the trauma instead of keeping it buried and festering.

"On the night before they were going to be officially

joined into our pack, the brothers attacked us in our sleep. They'd been living with the pack for a few weeks and knew everything about us. They targeted the weakest families first, slaughtering them one by one in the quiet of the night. None of us were the wiser until my strongest wolves were attacked. I heard the shouts, then smelled the smoke. My house was on fire, and all exits had been blocked."

Tears fell down my cheeks and I did my best to stay quiet. Foster's gaze was foggy, and I knew he wasn't present in the room as he continued to speak.

"We were a small pack. There were only thirty-four of us, including the childr—" Foster finally broke when the word got stuck in his throat.

I let go of his hand and wrapped my arms around him. "None of that was your fault, Foster. I know my words won't lessen your pain, but whoever those men were, they were sick and twisted sociopaths from the sounds of it. *They* are responsible for those lives lost, not you."

He stiffened under my hold, and his voice turned to ice. "No. I was the alpha. I was charged with their safety, and I failed. Every single one of my pack members died that night, Andie. By the time I smashed through one of the exits, the brothers were gone, and every other house was lit with flames. With burns all over my body, I lay in the snow, begging for death to take me, but I wasn't that lucky. I had to pay for their lives by living every day with the weight of their deaths on my shoulders."

I pulled back from the embrace and grabbed his chin, forcing him to meet my gaze. "You didn't die, because it wasn't your time. Blame had nothing to do with you surviving."

His eyes glossed over with tears that refused to fall. "You weren't there. You don't know."

"No, I wasn't, but I've seen glimpses of how much you're willing to fight for the people you care about. Your actions have shown me that you're a good man and, while this soulmate thing has been a lot to process since finding out, I'm even more glad that you found me after hearing your story."

Foster didn't budge. I knew he was having a hard time believing that I was telling the truth. I knew that if my words didn't change his mind that maybe my actions would.

It had only been a day since I'd met Foster, and I'd been asleep for most of that time, but regardless of not feeling the bond, my instincts trusted him. I'd always listened to the little nudges inside me, and I wasn't going to stop now.

I leaned forward, licking my lips, and my eyes darted to his. Foster had been forward in his feelings, and it was time I returned the sentiment.

Without overthinking my actions, I pressed my lips to his while gripping his forearm for support and dragged myself closer. My pulse raced when I kissed him softly and pulled back long enough to hear his sharp intake of breath.

One of his hands gently held my head, and his lips brushed over mine the second time. I opened to him and held his arm tighter when his tongue pushed forward. My other hand pressed against his chest. The warmth of his skin, the steady beat of his heart, and the firm pressure of his touch were burned into my mind.

I craved more of him with every stroke of his tongue that I eagerly matched. Yet, even as things heated up, the kiss wasn't about sexual need. The need for comforting and closeness ignited within me. I wanted nothing more than to soothe the sharp edges of the darkness he carried.

Heat rose to my cheeks when his hand moved down my back, forcing me closer to him, and I moaned from the length of his body lining up with mine.

The single sound had Foster going rigid underneath me. "I'm sorry."

I kept my face close to his, gripping his shirt. "For what?"

"Didn't I hurt you?"

"That noise wasn't from pain, Foster," I said, only slightly embarrassed.

"Oh."

My lips brushed over his again, hoping to show him how true my words were, but then I heard Charlie's and Beatrix's voices getting closer from outside.

Foster was already moving to sit up before I pulled back. His fingers grazed my cheek. "To be continued, then."

My skin flushed, and I nodded before glancing at the opening door.

Charlie's grin grew. "Well, hello you two."

I felt like I was being busted by my parents for having a boy in my room. Beatrix pushed forward, peering first at me and then Foster. He held her stare, but there was no sneering shared between them, which I counted as a win.

"Are you feeling better?" she asked me once she looked away from Foster.

"I am. I need to thank Camille for everything she did."

"She'd appreciate that. Now, we need to talk. I know this is only your second night here, but we don't have time to waste. Not with Moira having your necklace now." Beatrix took a seat on the chair opposite from us.

Charlie entered the living room, choosing to stand by her

fireplace. "Our saving grace is that Junie didn't just place your magic in some random object. You said the necklace was a moonstone, and when I told Beatrix that, she knew exactly which stone Junie used."

My eyes traveled to Beatrix, waiting for her to elaborate.

"Before we get to that, I'd like to say something else," she said, then she nodded at Foster. "I'm sorry for prodding you when I knew you were already too tightly strung from the bond. I tend to find enjoyment in testing others, and you were too easy of a target."

That wasn't exactly the apology I had been hoping Beatrix would give Foster, but he didn't seem upset by her choice of words.

"I accept and apologize as well," he said. "This is your coven, and I'll do my best to show restraint when you piss me off. I just want what is best for Andie."

I closed my eyes and rolled them at the same time. These two were terrible at apologies, but as long as they were getting along, I wouldn't push for something more.

Beatrix smirked. "As we all do. So, as Charlie was saying, the moonstone used to capture Andie's magic is an old coven heirloom. The stone was gifted to the first generation of Bishop witches from the Moon Goddess herself, which makes things all that more interesting considering the bond between the two of you."

"Seems as if my creator has known who my mate would be for longer than even *I* realized," Foster grumbled.

"She's the reason you arrived well before Andie, yes?" Beatrix asked.

Foster nodded. "She gave me Andie's scent. Roses and sage. My wolf followed the smell all the way here without question. We could only find the sage aroma when we arrived, which I assume came from Junie?"

"Witches don't pick up scents like you wolves do, but I would have to agree with your assumption. Most blood-related witches share more than just genes. It would make sense for them to carry similar smells within their magic," Beatrix answered.

"So, what about the necklace? What's so special about it being this particular moonstone?" I asked. I needed to know if there was still a chance of getting my magic back without it being tampered with by Moira. That blast of dark energy I'd been hit with was more than I wanted to ever experience again.

"Luna, the Moon Goddess, has gifted stones over the years that contain a sliver of her power," Beatrix explained. "They can be used to protect or heal, but they're only good for one use. Your ancestors must have known this would be a monumental moment in our history to have saved the moonstone all this time."

"I was only a child. How would Aunt Junie have known the importance of keeping my magic in an object so special?" I asked.

Charlie grinned, still leaning against the fireplace. "You'll find that our ancestors are never truly gone when you need them most. Once you have full access to your magic, there's an otherworldly sense that you get. That's your family, standing behind you."

My throat burned and I swallowed thickly. "Are you saying I could talk to my parents and aunt again?"

"Yes, but not whenever you want to. Though, you'll always be able to feel them. The more time that passes, you'll even learn to tell who's keeping watch," Beatrix answered.

My chest expanded while I tried to process that information. I'd missed my family so much that there was a physical ache inside me, one I'd considered a permanent part of me. Knowing I could have them back in any sense... That was everything to me.

"When can we go take my necklace back?" I asked.

Beatrix grimaced. "Now, that's more complicated unless you don't care about the number of witches who will die getting it back."

amaiya.com

19

———

FOSTER

Hearing that Andie's magic hadn't been stored in just any necklace, but a moonstone gifted directly from my creator… I wasn't sure how that made me feel. As open as I was to being bonded to a complete stranger, the thought that Luna had known what was to come and hadn't allowed me to prevent Andie's magic from being stolen pissed me the fuck off.

I was tasked with protecting Andie, yet I'd been set up to fail right from the start. If Andie couldn't feel the bond, we'd never fully share the same feelings. We needed her necklace to make that happen, and she deserved the magic that belonged to her. Most importantly, it should have never been stolen in the first place.

"Of *course* I care how many people could die by helping me," Andie said, responding to Beatrix's crude comment.

"Why do you assume witches will die? What about the contingency plans you mentioned?" I asked Beatrix before she could say anything to further upset my mate.

"Those plans only include keeping the coven safe, not

infiltrating a coven powered by dark energy that none of my witches want anything to do with. There's a reason none of us have gone after Moira all this time, even when we knew what she was dabbling with. She shares her family magic with two others that she keeps locked away in her coven. Nobody is even sure if they're women or men or what their relation is to Moira. What we do know is that she controls the Grimm family magic and uses it however she sees fit."

"Why haven't her ancestors stopped her?" I asked, knowing that the connection between those living and dead for witches was still very close.

"We're not sure why they haven't interfered, which is another reason for things being complicated. I've tried to glean information from my own line, but there's only so much they can tell us. We're all meant to walk our own path, and if too much is given away, it could cause a ripple effect amongst our worlds. Not in a good way, either. That's a shitstorm I don't want to be caught in the middle of."

That is why the Moon Goddess didn't give us more information. We must find it within ourselves to overcome the challenges we're going to face, my wolf said.

And what if the price of facing those challenges is too high to pay?

Whatever is meant to be will. You need to have faith.

"Faith" was a small word with a big meaning. It meant believing in something I couldn't prove. Something I couldn't retaliate against. Something that gave me hope. All things that had the power to crush me if I lost too much in the process.

I needed action to keep me from losing my shit. This conversation wasn't helping.

"So," I said, recapping, "Moira only has three witches

within her family line, making the potency of their magic stronger since there are so few of them. She, or they, have tainted their family magic, making what Moira is capable of unpredictable and dangerous. There seems to be no help from either your ancestors or Moira's. We're left trying to figure things out on our own, yet none of the witches want to face this challenge because there are too many risks, thanks to the dark magic. Have I gotten all of that right?"

The longer I spoke, the more my ire grew. If this had been a wolf pack discussing another dangerous pack, they wouldn't have been scared. They would have come together and fought for what was right. This was why I'd always believed witches were too selfish to be trusted. All too often, they only cared about themselves and not their coven as a whole.

Andie must have sensed my downward spiral, because she grabbed my hand, intertwining her fingers with mine and squeezed tightly.

"What if I didn't get my magic back? What would be so bad about letting Moira keep a necklace she likely can't break into thanks to this Moon Goddess?" Andie asked.

The idea of her never truly experiencing the bond made my chest restrict until breathing was nearly impossible.

Charlie moved from the fireplace and took a seat on the arm of the couch next to Andie. "Witches have long been hunted for their power. The reason we were attacked the day your father died was because another coven sought to take your family magic. When there are so few members left in an original line like yours, you become a target. At the time of the attack, it was only your father, Junie, and yourself. Beatrix had forced Junie into hiding, just as your parents had done to you and me when it began. Your father hadn't been as compliant. He refused to hide and leave the coven with one less defender."

He sounded like a warlock I could have gotten along with.

Charlie continued. "Junie helped us locate the people responsible after you and your mother had left. We hoped that if they were dead, then the two of you would come home, but that wasn't an option your mother was comfortable with, for obvious reasons. Instead, Junie did her best to teach you what she could during her short visits."

"What happened to Junie's magic when she died?" I asked, given Andie barely contained any inside herself.

"I have it," Beatrix answered. "I was there when she moved beyond the veil. I held her hand as she took her last breath and captured the energy before anything could happen to it."

Andie sucked in a breath and narrowed her eyes. "Why didn't you tell me that?"

"Because you didn't ask."

We'd gone this whole conversation without Beatrix acting superior. I should have known that had been too good to be true.

"If you have Junie's energy, then you need to give it to Andie," I said, doing my best to stay rational.

"Why? So the two of you can bond and leave and think that everything will be okay? I don't hand out happily-ever-afters," she replied with contempt.

Andie stood, fists at her sides. "You have no idea what you're talking about. I never asked for any of this, but I'm not a coward. I remember this coven. In my heart, this is home. I won't just leave if there's still a problem. Screw you for thinking so."

Charlie reached for her, but Andie shrugged her off. "I can't."

Andie went to the door, then she turned once more to sneer at Beatrix. "I thought you were someone I could trust, but if you can't do the same for me, then I don't belong here anymore."

Beatrix said nothing in response, and Andie slammed the door closed when she exited the house.

"What is wrong with you?" I demanded and stood to follow my mate.

"I need to protect the coven as a whole," Beatrix replied.

"That might be the case, but what you just said to her, that was low, even for you." I turned to Charlie. "I'll keep her safe tonight."

She nodded but said nothing.

I raced out the door to find my mate. I hated to say I despised witches when Andie was lumped into that category, but Beatrix was making it hard not to. They were all lucky that I'd finally taken Holden's advice to heart and wasn't tearing apart the coven on my way out.

Regardless of what had just gone down, I knew Andie still cared about this place and at least some of the people inside its walls. I had to proceed assuming we'd be right back here tomorrow, trying to work together again.

She's headed for the gate, my wolf said, and I picked up the pace.

When we found her, Andie's shoulders were slumped forward, and she was holding on to the gate with her head hanging down.

I approached slowly and gently touched her arms. "It's just me."

"Can we leave?" she asked in a quiet voice.

"Of course. We can go anywhere you want."

"Where did you stay before you sensed our bond?" she asked, and I really didn't want to tell her I'd slept mostly outside and kept my things in a storage unit. Instead, I just avoided answering.

"I know where we can go as long as you don't mind being around wolf shifters," I said.

She sighed. "That sounds a lot better than staying here."

Fucking Beatrix. She'd hurt my mate, and I wanted to break the witch in two, but taking care of Andie was more important. I took a steadying breath and turned Andie to me.

"I can run with you in my arms at a pretty quick pace and we'll get there a lot faster than walking, as long as you don't mind. Or I can try to call for a ride."

My words brought a spark of life back to her beautiful face. "As you are now or in your wolf form?"

I offered a small smile. "As I am now. My wolf is faster than I am, but he can't run on two legs. My shifter genes make me much faster than most on two feet."

I might be able to run only using my back legs. We've never tried. Maybe we should test it out, he said.

Not today, Wolf, I replied dryly even though I knew he was joking.

Andie took a step closer, and I wasted no time picking her up. She wrapped one arm behind my neck and connected her hands as she nestled against me.

A rumble I couldn't hold back vibrated through my chest, and she laughed.

"Is that a wolf thing or a Foster thing?" she asked.

"I'd like to say a Foster thing, but it's probably more of a mate thing," I answered when we stepped outside of the coven.

Night had fallen, but it was still warm out. Though, if Andie got cold while I was running, hopefully she'd just bury herself closer to me.

"Ready?" I asked her.

She glanced behind us and sighed. "I guess so."

"This doesn't mean you can't come back. There's nothing wrong with taking some time away to wrap your head around everything that's happened."

"Thank you for understanding. I need that right now," she said softly.

I nodded, then began to run under the thin streams of moonlight above us. Energy simmered over my exposed skin, reminding me there were still things I had to do with the wolves in the coming days.

There was going to be a new moon in a few days, and I knew that meant I would need to run with the pack and spend the night away from Andie. I wasn't thrilled with that, but I'd made a commitment to Holden in exchange for his help. I'd honor his wishes and be part of his pack.

I'd also yet to introduce myself, but I'd take care of that in the morning, assuming that Andie was going to want to stay the night away from the coven. Though maybe sleeping in the wolf's den wasn't what she had in mind, either.

"How long will it take us to get there like this?" she asked, her voice raised unnecessarily for my wolf ears.

"About twenty minutes. Rest your eyes. I'll slow down before we get there so you can get your bearings again."

She nodded and closed her eyes. I stood a little taller knowing that she trusted me so completely. I was a near-stranger to her, yet she rested in my arms, as vulnerable as could be.

A grin spread across my face while I raced through the forest, taking the familiar path to the pack. For the first time since my family had been destroyed, a sense of rightness settled within me. This was where I belonged. Right here with Andie, keeping her safe.

I intended to do that until my dying breath, even if she never got her magic back.

20

ANDIE

I had only been at the coven for twenty-four hours before I'd had enough. My first freak-out upon arrival had been just the tip of the iceberg. After knowing Beatrix had messed with my emotions, learning I had a soulmate, seeing my house ransacked, losing the only thing that might make me feel whole again, getting hurt to the point I probably should have died, and then hearing Beatrix say she'd been keeping my aunt's magic from me... I couldn't take anymore.

Even though Foster had been a lot, he'd been the one with whom I felt safest. Given that I knew Charlie—sort of—I realized that seemed weird, but I needed to get away from the witches, and Charlie wouldn't have been able to do that for me.

I needed a moment to breathe and think and feel however I wanted without the heaviness I'd left behind at the coven.

I thought I could handle my life being turned upside

down merely because I knew in my heart that being a witch was truly who I was, but I'd been wrong.

The farther Foster carried me away from the coven, the more tension my body released. His heart beat steadily beneath my ear, and his heated skin kept me warm while I held on tighter to him, needing his closeness.

Regardless of not feeling an explosive connection with him like he had when he saw me, I was beginning to realize that I didn't need that moment of recognition to know the bond was there.

The lure I felt to Foster, the way he made my insides burn with just one look, the euphoria of kissing him, all of that combined was enough to know that I wanted—no, *needed*—to know more about him. And that he would always be someone I could count on.

That seemed irrational to my human-raised mind, but the supernatural part of me was over the damn moon that he'd found me.

While I wasn't head-over-heels in love with Foster, I was open to wherever this road was leading us.

He slowed his pace, and I loosened my grip on him, peeking out around us. I still only saw the same trees that surrounded the coven, which made me believe we were in the same section of forest. That surprised me, given witches and wolves hadn't always gotten along.

"It's about a five-minute walk to the main house from here," Foster said when he started to set me down.

"Just enough time for me to get my legs back. I have to admit, it took a lot out of me to run toward the barrier when we left."

Foster's hands stayed close to me while I stretched. "Do you still feel the dark magic inside you?"

His voice was panicked, but I shook my head. "No, just sore. I did a lot of hiking in Montana, but apparently, not enough to prepare me for getting blasted in the back and everything I went through last night."

A growl rumbled from Foster. "I should have been there."

"Yeah, probably, but it's done now. Everything I ever owned was destroyed or stolen," I said with a grimace.

Foster grabbed my hand. "We'll get you some things tomorrow, so you don't have to keep borrowing clothes from Charlie."

"Shit. I never called my work. With everything that happened, I forgot to tell them I wouldn't be coming back." I hadn't been scheduled to work earlier, or the day after, but I had said I'd help out if needed since my boss had left for her own family emergency.

"I'm assuming you don't have your phone?" Foster asked.

I shook my head. "It hasn't turned on since I was leaving work and tried to call for a ride."

"Don't worry about it. We'll get everything taken care of in the morning. It's too late over there to make a call anyway."

"Why are you so calm right now?" I asked.

He stared up at the stars above. "Because that's what you need. It's your turn to scream at people," he said with a smirk.

"Fair enough." I chuckled.

"Now, if one of the wolves looks at you the wrong way, then you might see the me from last night. I want to preemptively apologize for that, but I wouldn't actually be sorry for showing them you belong to me."

Holy shit. Why did I find that so hot? He was possessive as hell, but even still, there wasn't a single thing about him that scared me. Maybe that was bad, and I was too overwhelmed to see it yet, but I was choosing to believe in the bond between us. To believe that when he said things like that to me with such conviction, no truer words had ever been spoken.

"I guess we'll just have to wait and see what happens," I finally said while we continued walking through the forest.

There were no roads that I could see. Just dirt walking paths like the well-worn one we were currently on. I wasn't sure how the pack got in and out, but the farther we went, the more at home I felt. There was a sense of familiarity about these woods, even though I was certain I'd never been here.

The tingles of energy inside me stirred, and I glanced down at my hands, but neither of them was glowing. The pulse continued inside me, keeping a steady beat that no longer frightened me. Instead, I yearned for the moment when I'd be able to truly unleash the magic I was supposed to have.

A gravel road finally appeared. I looked right, then left and saw lights. "Is that the pack?"

Foster nodded. "I've only been here a few times and have only seen the main house, but the territory spans over several thousand acres. This is only the front portion of their property."

"Why would they have this so close to town?" I asked, thinking the wolves would be more concerned with privacy.

"Convenience, mostly. From what I understood, a decent amount of the wolves have homes downtown and jobs there. This was a happy medium in keeping everyone as close as possible. A city pack like this wouldn't have been my first choice, given where I grew up, but it works."

I gave his hand a squeeze, guilt rising inside me that he was only somewhere he wouldn't normally have been because of me. I opened my mouth to say something, but the details of the house came into view, and I lost all other thought.

It was a monstrosity of a cabin, more like a mansion with big, open windows on the second level, log siding, and beautiful tree trunks used as supports to the expansive upper deck. A shiver ran up my spine, and I let out a small sigh.

"One hell of a house, huh?" Foster asked.

"You could say that."

The front door opened, and the man I'd seen with Foster earlier that day stepped out. He was older, with auburn hair and fine wrinkles on his face, but as he folded his muscled arms over his chest, I knew his age made no difference in his strength.

"Holden, this is Andie," Foster said when we approached.

Holden grinned at me. "It's lovely to formally meet you, Andie. What brings the two of you by?"

"Andie needed a break from the coven," Foster explained. "I was hoping you had those accommodations set up for me that you mentioned before and that we could stay for the night."

Holden tilted his head and looked down at Foster. "This isn't a hotel, Foster. I welcomed you into this pack with certain expectations. Are you ready to meet those?"

"I am. I'll introduce myself to the pack tomorrow during

breakfast, and I'll be part of the new moon run when it's time," Foster replied.

His voice was rough, and I hated that this was so hard for him. Understandable, after everything he'd told me earlier, though it further proved my reasoning for trusting him. He was sacrificing a lot to be here with me. Hopefully, I could find a way to be there for him in return.

Holden grinned. "Good news. You don't have to wait to meet the pack until tomorrow. We actually had a meeting tonight. You tripped our perimeter sensors just as it was finishing up, so I asked everyone to stay a bit longer. Follow me."

Holden turned for the door and I tugged on Foster's hand. "You don't have to do this for me. We can go back to the coven. I'm already feeling better."

He shook his head. "I'm not only doing this for you. I need to for my wolf and myself. We've been running from the past for too long."

"Can I do anything to help?" I asked.

"Just having you at my side is more than enough. I'll have to tell them who you are, but Holden has a good pack here. We can trust them. It's the only reason I joined when I realized you were going to need all the help you could get."

Holden was still waiting at the door, watching us. I wanted to continue this conversation, but not with an audience.

"I have no objections. I trust your instincts, Foster."

Foster sucked in a sharp breath at my words, but I nudged him forward. He squeezed my hand and whispered, "Thank you," in my ear as we approached the porch.

I smiled and nodded in reply as we entered the cabin through the double doors. In front of us was an open living room with a high ceiling that was accented by wooden beams and an intricate metal chandelier that had hand-forged metal vines and leaves interlacing between the lights.

The second level had a balcony that curved around, likely leading to the upper deck I had seen from the outside. There were four black leather couches that created an open square in the center of the living room and a large, stone fireplace on the wall nearest to them.

Off to the right appeared to be a dining room, and I couldn't see anything beyond that as Holden walked toward a hallway at the back of the welcoming room.

Every wall we passed was lined with wood planks. I'd have thought the oak would get overwhelming, but as we continued through the house, the varying shades grew on me.

"Just out here," Holden said when we approached a set of glass doors that led to another porch spanning the entire backside of the house.

Outdoor furniture covered most of the area except for where the six-foot-long barbeque was set up with what seemed like nearly everything I'd find in an indoor kitchen.

Foster gripped my hand tighter when we got to the edge of the deck. I glanced ahead and saw an open field with about fifty people standing in front of a small podium.

"Oh, you're not cruel enough to make him stand up there, are you?" I asked Holden.

The alpha's answering grin told me he was indeed. "Foster made a promise, and I intend to hold him to it, but your concern is noted."

"It'll be fine," Foster said, but the tense tone of his voice wasn't convincing.

I glanced back at Holden. "I can go with him?"

He nodded. "Absolutely."

As we got closer, all eyes present were on us and the voices quieted into murmurs.

"Is this everyone who lives here?" I asked.

"No, my pack is spread out. We have a lot of territory to protect, so I don't require all members to return for meetings, but there's a video feed set up right over there." Holden pointed to a tripod I hadn't noticed before.

"How many pack members do you have in total?" I asked before we approached the podium.

"Nearing three hundred," he answered with pride lacing his words.

"That's a lot of people to manage on your own," I noted.

Holden winked. "I don't do it on my own. I have a team who helps me."

Of course he did. I wanted to ask more questions, because this whole pack life intrigued me, but we'd reached the podium. It was time for me to be there for Foster.

I turned him toward me. "Are you ready?"

"I am." His voice was full of confidence this time, and all signs of the anxiety that I'd seen before was gone.

"I'll be right at your side."

He leaned forward and kissed my forehead. "And that's the only reason I'm ready."

21

FOSTER

Stepping up to the podium was easier than I'd thought it would be. When Andie had helped remind me of why I was doing this, the conviction inside me had grown stronger.

Andie deserved the best version of me. The one who was still holding on to the past was not that. I wasn't going to forget the pack I'd lost, but I was going to stop fighting my way back into another that not only accepted me, but that I accepted in return.

With Andie by my side, I lifted my head and stared into the crowd of men, women, and children. None of them seemed surprised to see me, which also made things easier.

I took a steadying breath and moved closer to the stand. "Hello. As I assume most of you already know, I'm Foster Kline. I've been in L.A. for a while now thanks to a nudge from our creator to go searching for my mate."

I nodded to Andie. She blushed and waved awkwardly, making me smile.

"She's a witch. I know that can bring its own troubles,

but right now, she's being targeted. I won't lie to you and pretend I joined your pack because living near the big city was where I wanted to be. I joined because for the first time in many years, I found another alpha I felt I could trust and depend on. Though, that isn't all. I need your help in keeping my mate safe. I know that's selfish of me to ask, given that I've only just arrived, but I promise to stay and earn my keep if you'll have me."

I paused, waiting for someone to respond to my honesty. The eerie silence was weighing down on my chest, so I finished.

"I don't know what tomorrow will bring, and I understand if my request is too much, but I'm desperate enough to ask you to consider offering your help. I'll be splitting my time between here and the coven, but I look forward to getting to know you all. If you have any questions for me, I'll be around tomorrow morning. Thank you."

I moved back with Andie, passing Holden when he stepped up to address the pack. "That's it for this month. Any other updates will be sent through the messaging system, but one final note. I expect each of you to keep our new pack member's business to yourself. I won't force any of you to fight for the witches, but just know it might come to a point where I ask for volunteers, just as Foster has. I know my visit to the vampires didn't go as planned, but this time, we'll be more prepared. I assure you."

The pack began to part, but a few of them headed toward us. I had hoped for an evening with just myself and Andie before the questions started, but I should have known better.

Holden grinned and clasped my shoulder. "Honesty was

the right choice. They would have seen through any other bullshit."

"I figured as much. Now we'll see if that backfires."

He gave my shoulder a tighter squeeze. "I think you're going to be pleasantly surprised with the members of this pack. Most of them aren't even going to care that you're here."

Andie snorted, then covered her mouth. "I'm sorry, but that's awesome."

Holden winked at her. "You see, Foster has only known the serious me. The one who has to be cautious with those outside of his pack, but now that I've tied him down, he's about to learn a thing or two from me."

"I think I'm going to enjoy that more than him," Andie replied, nudging me with her elbow.

"But business first. I want you both to meet some of my team leaders. This is my beta Mack," Holden said, gesturing to the man nearest to him.

He was wideset in the shoulders with dark, shaved hair, light golden skin, and a wide smile. "Nice to meet you, Foster. Holden's told me plenty already."

I shook his extended hand. "Wish I could say the same. Now that I think about it, Holden hasn't told me anything about any of you."

"Some things you have to learn yourself," Holden said before gesturing to a few more people. "This is Lawson, Piper, and Colby. One or more of them is always on site at the pack house and will know where to find me or Mack if you need anything. Our other team leaders are offsite. We own an apartment building that one of them runs and then a few small businesses in town that the others oversee."

I shook Lawson's hand first, noting his dark gaze, tense jaw, and copper skin.

"Welcome to the pack," he said after giving my hand a hard squeeze.

"I look forward to making it home," I replied, getting the feeling he wasn't going to make things as easy on me as Holden had.

I noticed Piper had an uncanny similarity to Holden when she approached me. Same auburn hair and light-green eyes, but her slight nose and thin lips were the opposite of Holden's.

She nodded at me and then Andie. "It's good to meet both of you."

Andie smiled. "Same. I wasn't allowed to go beyond the barrier when I was young, but it's nice to see how close you all are to the coven."

Holden scoffed. "Beatrix bought the land for her coven right out from under me. I intended to extend the pack, but she beat me to the sale and built her coven there just to piss me off."

I shook my head. That sounded just like the witch I'd been getting to know.

Last was Colby. He bypassed me and reached for Andie's hand, grabbing it and bowing before her. "Welcome to our pack."

I snarled and stepped between them, breaking his hold with ease. "You don't touch her without her permission."

"I was just being friendly," Colby said with a straight face, but there was a glint to his hazel eyes I didn't like.

Holden pulled Colby back with a firm jerk, grabbing him by the back of the neck. "Apologize. Now."

Colby's already pale, white skin turned to ash when he met my fiery glare. "I'm sorry. I was just—"

"Not to me. To *my* mate."

Colby gulped as Holden released him. "I apologize for touching you, Andie."

"Apology accepted," Andie said softly.

"The three of you go make sure nobody needed anything after the meeting. Mack, come with me to show our new guests around," Holden said, his tone leaving no room for argument.

Holden's quick action made me respect him even more. He knew when to be relaxed, but he also knew when to stop lines from being crossed. I could already tell he wasn't everyone's best friend, but he was well versed in garnering respect from his pack, just like he'd managed to do with me.

Once the other three wolves were gone, Holden turned to me and Andie. "I'm sorry. Colby is new to our leadership team. He means well, but he's the youngest of us and the one who likes to joke the most. He just doesn't always remember the appropriate time for that."

My arm wrapped around Andie's shoulder. "As long as he doesn't do it again, there's no harm done."

Mack shook his head while chuckling. "Yeah, I'm pretty sure he pissed his pants during all that. He won't cross you again. Not with all that alpha power flowing through you. One thing our wolves respect is rank and even if you're not in charge, they'll proceed with caution around you."

"I'm not here to lead. I hope you told them that," I said.

Holden nodded. "I did, but some of them won't be able to help how they act toward you. You'll have to learn to be okay with that."

I wanted to argue that he was wrong, but I knew that would be pointless. Now that I'd let my alpha power out, it was hard to contain. Knowing I might need it to fuel me later on, I wasn't going to bother trying to lock it down again.

"Want to see where our wolves work out?" Mack asked.

"Of course."

Andie yawned, and I quickly changed my answer.

"Actually, can we see the housing and where we might be able to get some food? Andie was hurt earlier today, and she hasn't eaten. I can come see everything once we've gotten settled if that works?"

Holden's brows pinched together. "How badly? Beatrix made it seem like whatever you were doing was going to be quick and simple."

"It was supposed to be," said Andie, "but the witches after me were waiting for us when we arrived. I was headed to the portal to leave, but one of them hit me in the back with dark magic."

"Shit, are you okay?" Mack asked.

Andie nodded. "Just tired now."

"It's understandable why you needed a break then. Just know, you're always welcome here, Andie. Even without Foster. Your connection to him makes you one of us," Holden said.

His words loosened a knot in my chest that I hadn't even known was there.

You made the right choice trusting this alpha, my wolf said.

It wasn't easy.

Nothing good in life usually is.

Touché, Wolf.

"Thank you, Holden," Andie said with a grin and another yawn.

"Food, then the cabin. Come on, you two," Mack said, turning to head back to the main house.

We followed him and Holden back inside, then they took us down another hallway. The all-wood home was more welcoming than I'd expected with all of the windows and open spaces.

Even as we entered the kitchen, the ceilings were high, and more windows wrapped around to where a long dinner table sat.

"As you see, we have two fridges. The one on the left is only for people who cook. Take anything from there and you'll find one of them at your door within the hour," Mack said, then he laughed. "Kidding. Mostly. The one on the right is all prepared food that you can take whenever you want. You can always find sandwiches, salads, soups to heat up, and snacks."

Mack opened the doors to reveal stacks of food, all wrapped in deli paper or packed in plastic containers.

Holden pointed to a white board next to the fridge. "If you have any special requests, write them here and usually they'll be taken into consideration unless you get too picky and then the chefs will make your life hell. Ask Lawson about that sometime."

"Noted," I said, then I reached into the fridge. "Ham, turkey, or roast beef?" I asked Andie.

"Actually, I'll take one of those salads with chicken, please." She nudged me aside, reaching for her own food.

I caught Mack's and Holden's grins as she made herself right at home.

"Non-perishable snacks are in these cabinets. Everything in here is free game. Just don't be an asshole and take hordes of anything to your cabin. Unless something sits for weeks, it's always restocked." Mack reached his hand out to me again. "My part of the tour is done for the night unless you get bored later. I'll have Holden text you my number in case you need anything else."

I gave him a firm shake. "Thank you, Mack."

He nodded and waved at Andie on his way toward the back of the house.

"To the cabins?" Holden asked.

Andie and I both nodded, following him out the front doors. We went around to the left and entered back into the forest.

I could hear motors running and asked about them.

"Some of the homes are farther out than others. We have a couple dozen ATVs that people use to get around when they don't feel like running," Holden replied.

"I didn't mind running," Andie said with a laugh.

"Because you didn't do any of the actual running," I replied dryly.

"Exactly."

I like this side of her. She's getting more comfortable with us, my wolf said.

Or it could just be because we're not at the coven.

He sighed. *Can't you ever be positive?*

I wanted to say *no,* but I ended the private conversation when we arrived at a cabin that I assumed was for us. Well, me, but I wanted Andie to feel at home here as well.

"Everything inside is new. This is one of our guest cabins. Depending on what your living situation is going to look like, we can look at other options later on," Holden explained.

I read between the lines, and I knew Andie would have as well. If things got serious quickly between the two of us, we'd need our own house that could be a home. Not a small one-bedroom space.

For now, it would work, though.

"Thank you, Holden. For everything," I said.

"We're glad to have you, and I'm sure your wolf is glad to be done sleeping in the woods," he replied with a wink.

As he walked away, Andie lightly punched me. "You always sleep in the woods?"

"It's what animals do, Andie. It's not a big deal." I opened the door.

I found the light switch easily and inhaled deeply, noticing a window open that was bringing fresh air into the unused cabin. On our right was a small dining table with a minifridge on top of a storage cabinet behind it. On the left was one couch and a moderate-sized TV secured to the wall. In front of us was a short hallway with two doors. From where I stood, I could see one was the bathroom and the other a bedroom with a king-sized bed.

Andie was eyeing the bedroom as well with an odd look on her face.

"I'll sleep on the couch," I offered.

She blinked and waved a hand. "Nonsense. We're adults. Not uncontrollable teenagers. We can share a bed without having…sex."

I hid a grin when she stumbled over even saying "sex." "Yes, we sure can."

One day we'll share more than a bed with her, my wolf said.

One day, I agreed.

It wasn't as if I hadn't ever been serious with a man, but thinking about Foster and a bed and what that bed could lead to... I wanted to stick my head in a freezer before I flushed to an embarrassing shade of red.

With my salad gripped tightly between my hands, I followed Foster to the table. He set his sandwich down and began to unwrap the paper around it. I popped the lid off my container then frowned. I had no fork, and there wasn't a kitchen in this cabin.

Foster reached behind him and opened a drawer beneath the mini fridge. He held a wrapped plastic fork up and smirked. "Need this?"

"Maybe." I snatched the utensil before he could tease me with it.

His grin spread as he lifted his roast beef sandwich, taking his first bite. "Damn, that's good," he muttered with a full mouth.

I poked at my salad, grabbing lettuce, chicken, and a cherry tomato in one go. It was too much for a single bite, but I was famished and didn't care. I shoveled the food in without a care that Foster was watching me intently while he chewed slowly.

His eyes heated my already warm skin, and I couldn't stop the images of us sharing that bed tonight from popping into my head. Would he sleep under the covers? Did I want him to?

Soulmates aside, I was still a woman. The thought of running my fingers over his muscled arms and searching out the remainder of the tattoos covering his body was a tantalizing one. Though I couldn't completely forget that this wasn't a date, and I wasn't with just any guy.

Foster would one day be more than a boyfriend. I didn't know why that thought made me want to take things slower with him, but the importance of what was to come made this relationship seem worth taking my time with.

We ate in comfortable silence, only the sound of our chewing echoing through the room. Being with Foster, while overwhelming at times, was as easy as breathing.

At first, that thought had terrified me. Everything about what I'd been exposed to over the last two days had done that, but while the coven reminded me of home, this was the first time I'd felt at peace since leaving work.

Foster crumpled the wrapper from his sandwich and groaned. "I needed that."

I wiped my mouth with a napkin and eyed my half-eaten salad. I'd thought my stomach had been starving, but maybe I'd been hungry for something more than food.

When I looked up at Foster, his dark-blue eyes were pulsing, and his hands wrapped around the edge of the table.

I licked my lips and glanced down, partially ashamed,

because even the growing tension between us was appealing to me.

Foster's finger lifted my chin back up, curving softly and urging me closer to him. His eyes were still dark when I stared into them, and he was breathing heavier.

He stroked his thumb over the corner of my lips, then pulled away with a sliver of lettuce on the pad of his finger.

My first instinct was to grab his thumb and run my tongue over it, but that wasn't me. At least, it hadn't been who I was before coming here and meeting him.

Foster rubbed his hand over his jean-clad thigh, then stood and grabbed our garbage. "If you're finished, I'll clean this up."

I nodded, afraid to speak.

What the shit was wrong with me? Maybe I was feeling effects of the bond and didn't realize it. Or maybe now that I was truly alone with Foster, it was a lot harder to ignore how attractive he really was.

Everything from his long, dark hair to the sexy facial hair and the thick muscles I could see rippling beneath his grey T-shirt was tempting.

Maybe I needed to go back to the coven. I didn't think I was going to survive the night sharing a bed with Foster without doing something I absolutely wouldn't regret. Of course, I knew that made no sense, which was why I was still sitting at the table with my head in my hands.

Foster had other plans, though.

He shocked the hell out of me when I was suddenly in his arms, my face mere inches from his. "I'm a wolf shifter," he grumbled.

I chuckled. "Color me shocked."

"I sense things most people can't." There was a tick in his cheek as he forced the words out.

I didn't understand what he meant at first, but when I realized that he could "sense" me, I nearly died in his arms.

I turned away from him and threw an arm over my face, but Foster wasn't having any of that.

"Do you feel the bond now?" he asked, eyes bouncing between my terrified stare and my panting chest.

"I don't know. I just know there's something more that I'm feeling that wasn't there before," I admitted.

Foster's grip on me tightened, bringing me closer to him. I sucked in a breath and tilted my head to the side, raising my hand to grip his neck.

My nails dug into his skin, and he turned for the bedroom. The anticipation had excitement spreading through me and my inner muscles clenching.

Foster kicked the door all the way open and in two long strides, he laid me on the mattress, leaving my legs dangling over the edge. I'd thought he was going to back away, but instead, he leaned forward, placing both of his hands above my shoulders.

"Do you want me to leave, Andie?" he murmured, looking down on me with his lips only inches from mine.

Before I could think too much, I lifted my legs, and my ankles locked around his thighs. "I'd rather you stay."

His lips crashed down onto mine, burning my skin with need as I hungrily kissed him back. My hands got lost in his hair, and I brought him closer while our tongues danced to a song that only we could hear.

I didn't know what I'd expected, but I couldn't deny the growing need inside me. The feel of Foster pressed against me, his heat branding my skin, the taste of him on my tongue… All of it called to me, and there was no turning away.

I needed Foster like I needed my next breath of air.

His thumbs stroked over my cheeks, and he adjusted his feet that were still on the ground. The movement aligned him perfectly between my legs and the twitching of his hard length had my hips drawing up.

"So beautiful," Foster whispered over my lips, then he kissed down my neck, swirling his tongue over my collarbone.

My chest expanded, soaking him in, and I arched into his embrace, my hands moving from his hair to his shoulders.

Foster lifted me up, moving us farther onto the bed. "I didn't bring you here to do this."

"I know you didn't. I trust you, Foster." My words were simple, but I hoped he knew how much I meant them.

It didn't matter that I'd only just met him, or that I hadn't experienced something soul-shattering when I'd first seen him. This slow build of yearning between us was exactly what I needed.

I reached up for the hem of his shirt. "Let's get ready for bed."

The tick in his cheek was back, and his eyes darkened to nearly black when he reached one arm back, pulling his shirt off with one tug.

My core clenched when my eyes roamed over his upper half. The tattoos that covered his arms extended over his chest and stomach. I lifted my hand, letting my fingers trail over the black and grey images, the biggest of them being a wolf's head, a compass, and several peony flowers.

Foster's skin rippled under my appraising touch, then he lowered himself and nipped at the sensitive skin on my neck. His hands slid under my shirt but didn't go any higher than my ribs, even as I wiggled beneath him.

I gripped his head and brought his mouth to mine, desperately needing his kiss. Our tongues began another dance, and the sultry taste of him had my hips lifting once again.

One of his hands brushed my hair back as he rested on one elbow. "Andie."

He said my name like a warning.

"What's wrong?" I asked.

"As much as it pains me to say this, I thought we were getting ready for bed."

I reached between us, gripping his hard length. "We are."

His chest rumbled. "I'm trying to be chivalrous, and you're making it very hard."

"I can feel that." I smirked and squeezed him again before adding, "In my defense, you're the one who brought us into the bedroom."

He grimaced, which I took as his agreement that I was right before pushing on his chest. I rolled us over and situated myself on top of him.

Foster's eyes narrowed. He was an alpha. He probably didn't like not being in charge, but if him being in charge meant calling off what he—or maybe I—had started, then I was firing him. I still wanted to take things slowly with him, but that didn't mean we couldn't *do* anything.

Shamelessly, I rubbed against him and leaned down to kiss him again. His hands gripped my hips, pushing my center over his cock. I moaned into the kiss and nipped at his lips.

I lifted enough that I could take off my shirt, but when the fabric got tangled around my arms, he leaned his head forward, sucking on my belly button before regaining control.

Not only were our positions reversed again, but my hands were still trapped, and half of my face was covered. So much for being sexy and graceful.

Foster lifted my shirt so I could see him, then he twisted the fabric tighter around my hands. "Leave those there," he demanded.

I thought I'd been turned on before, but holy shit. I squeezed my legs together, needing the pressure when I felt my underwear getting wet.

Foster inhaled, and when his eyes met mine again, I nearly exploded from my waiting orgasm. His gaze was dark and heated and only for me, trailing down my body, then back up to my face again.

"I want to cherish every moment with you," he said. "I don't want to rush anything with you and allow you to feel any regret."

My heart crushed a little when I thought he was calling this off, but then he continued.

"But I won't leave my mate in this state."

Hell yes, I thought.

I lifted my head as far as I could, and Foster met me in the middle. He kissed me senseless, then pulled away, moving his lips between my breasts and making his way south.

My arms tried to reach for him, but he lifted his head and growled. "Those stay up or I'm sleeping on the couch."

I glared at him, but on the inside, I was bouncing around like a child, ready for whatever he was going to give me.

With focused effort, I kept my arms where Foster wanted

them and writhed beneath him. His tongue swirled over each of my hips while his fingers tugged at my jeans.

I lifted up to help, thankful for the brand-new matching bra and underwear set Charlie had tucked into her drawer. The black lace rolled down my legs and Foster growled, his lips nearly where I wanted them.

He kissed each of my inner thighs, spreading them apart with calloused hands. His thumb lightly stroked my slit and I bucked into his touch.

"So eager," he murmured.

"Your fault," I groaned, thrashing my head to the side.

The sight of my misery must have triggered something in Foster, because after that, there were no more complaints. I gasped then moaned when his tongue flicked against my clit.

Foster continued his delectable assault by adding his fingers into the mix. The pressure from his touch and tongue had me on the cusp of release within seconds, but I wasn't ready for it to be over, and I had a feeling Foster wasn't going to let us take things too far tonight.

I admired and appreciated that, because no matter how turned on I was, taking things slow was important to me.

I bit the inside of my cheek, and my hands turned to fists above me. My skin tingled with ecstasy, and I arched my back, only able to focus on the pleasure coursing through me like I'd never known before.

Foster's chest vibrated with another rumble, and he lifted my legs higher in the air before running his tongue from end to end of my center.

Shivers wracked my body, and when he curled two fingers inside me, hitting that perfect spot, I saw stars. I brought my hands low enough to muffle my screams while I bucked beneath him, quivering in satisfaction.

When I came down from my high, Foster was kissing his way up my stomach. He lifted my arms and grinned. "That's how I always want to leave you."

"I'll be dead in weeks if that's true," I murmured.

"I'll always bring you back to me." Foster winked and stood. "Be right back."

I nodded, already missing his skin against mine but unable to move after that epicness. I lay on the bed in nothing more than my bra while I listened to his footfalls entering the bathroom and the faucet turning on.

He quickly brushed his teeth, then I heard him re-enter the room. I flinched when an unexpected heat covered my center. Foster had brought a warm washcloth back with him and was cleaning me up.

How could this be real? Not only had I never had a man give me an orgasm that powerful, but I'd never had one be so concerned with only my needs.

I knew then that even if I never got my magic back, if I never felt the true connection of the bond that was supposed to be between us, I was never going to regret this moment with Foster or any other that I hoped for in the future.

23

FOSTER

Sleep was elusive for me while I held Andie in my arms. Morning had arrived, but my mind was still stuck on the night before.

I'd known Andie was attracted to me, but I hadn't expected her to have wanted me as much as she had. My instincts had been to have my way with her, especially when she was so willing, but I knew that cherishing each moment with her was going to mean so much more than rushing things with her merely because I had the opportunity.

Andie was my mate. It was my job to know her better than she knew herself, and sometimes that meant torturing both of us for the greater good. The thought of her waking up with regrets this morning if we'd had sex was enough to keep me in check.

You did the right thing. I agree that this will only bring the two of you closer, my wolf said.

Andie chose that moment to nuzzle closer to me, and I brushed the back of my hand lightly over her arm.

Her head was on my chest, and her long strands of hair

were spread out on the pillow she hadn't once used. Our legs were tangled together, and I sighed in contentment.

This was what I'd been missing all my life. I'd do whatever I had to in order to make sure we had a lifetime of mornings like this.

The glow of the rising sun peeked through the blinds, shining right into Andie's eyes. She groaned and lifted an arm up to cover her face.

"What time is it?" she muttered.

"No clue, but I know it's after seven since the sun is up," I answered.

After I'd cleaned her up the night before, I'd dressed her in my grey shirt, which was now riding up on her hips.

I slipped out from under her and kissed her chastely. When I got out of bed, she jutted her lower lip out, making me want to lean back down and bite it.

"I know lying here in bed all day would be preferable, at least to me, but we should probably get you back to the coven," I said. "Not only for clothes, but to let them know you're okay."

Andie didn't have a phone, and I didn't have any of the witches' contact information. I wasn't sure if Beatrix would be willing to come to the pack or not, but I wanted to keep the measly amount of peace we had built before the argument that led to us leaving. I wouldn't be able to do that if I kept Andie away for days at a time.

"Beatrix isn't the same person I remembered as a child," Andie said.

"I'm not surprised by that. I know how she acted yesterday was unacceptable, but a part of me wonders if she sometimes doesn't know when a little empathy is needed in certain conversations. As much as she's pissed me off, I can't deny that she does seem to truly care about her coven."

Andie huffed. "If she cared so much, then why wouldn't she have told me about my aunt's magic? Why wouldn't she have offered it to me the moment she realized I didn't have mine?"

"I don't have the answers to those questions. Only Beatrix does. You might not like her right now, but we need her," I said, sounding just like Holden. Though I didn't consider that a bad thing.

Andie grimaced. "What happened to the man who shoved her against a wall when she blasted me with magic?"

I moved back onto the bed, the mattress dipping beneath my weight when I leaned closer to Andie. "He's still here. If Beatrix still chooses to withhold your family magic from you, she'll know there's a price to pay for that choice, but we won't know if things have changed unless we show up."

She looked up at me with eyes full of innocence and complete trust. "Okay."

My chest felt like someone had punched it just from the one word.

"I'll take a shower and then we'll go." I kissed her again then stood back up.

She scrambled to the edge of the bed, sitting up on her knees, and snagged my wrist, pulling me toward her again. Her arms wrapped around my neck and her tongue demanded entry into my mouth that I gladly granted. My fingers tangled with her hair, and I angled her head to deepen the unexpected kiss.

When she pulled back, she grinned. "Thank you."

I raised a brow. "For?"

"For knowing what I need. For finding your calm. For being here."

"Always," I said, then I headed out of the room before I got back in the bed. If I let that happen, it would be hours before we left the pack.

Would that be such a bad thing? my wolf asked.

No, but it's not what Andie needs right now and considering what she just thanked me for, I need to keep my mind clear.

I'm not sure she's ready for what's to come.

I sighed, knowing my wolf was right. *We'll keep her safe.*

As I thought the words, I hoped like hell they would be proven true. If anything happened to Andie, I would burn the whole world to ash.

AFTER I'D SHOWERED AND WE'D BOTH CHANGED INTO THE SAME clothes from the night before, I went in search of Holden. I wanted to be respectful and let him know we were leaving since I wasn't sure I'd be back tonight.

He was sitting on the porch, whittling on some wood, when we arrived at the pack house. "Good morning."

Andie smiled and waved. "Good morning to you."

"We're going to go check in at the coven. I'm not sure when I'll be back—unless you need something," I said.

Holden set down the owl he was carving and stood. "I understand you have things to do. You coming here to let me know you're taking off is appreciated and noted. Do what you have to, and I'll find you if we need you."

I met his outstretched hand, and we shook as I nodded my head. "Thank you, Holden."

"Anytime, Son."

The way "son" had so easily rolled off his tongue had me tensing. It had been a long time since anyone called me "son." My father had died the night of the attack on my old pack. There wasn't a part of me that didn't miss him or my mother.

Andie was staring up at me when we walked back down the stairs. I didn't want her to worry, so I picked her up without saying anything, enjoying the sound of her squeals.

"Is this okay?" I asked.

"Absolutely."

We raced through the forest and, just like the night before, Andie kept her head tucked against my chest while I watched our surroundings. I could sense members of the pack near, but none of them came toward us while we continued to the coven.

When the trees thinned, warmth from the sun shined down on us and I slowed my pace. The road leading to the witches was only a few feet ahead and I stopped.

"Are you ready for this?" I asked.

Andie nodded. "You were right earlier. Tensions are high for everyone. I can't hold how Beatrix acted last night against her, but I won't deny the time away was exactly what I needed. Thank you for bringing me to your pack."

I tightened my arms around her and brought my lips down on hers. Her scent of roses and sage enveloped me, and I pulled back to put her on her feet before we got carried away again.

She straightened her wrinkled shirt, then surprised me by grabbing my hand. We walked the rest of the way out of the forest and across the road to the coven barrier.

I still wasn't able to get through on my own, but Beatrix

was waiting for us anyway. She stepped outside of the shield when we approached.

Her eyes appraised Andie, then she met my stare. "Thank you for keeping her safe."

"No thanks needed," I replied.

She made an odd noise with her throat, then gave Andie her full attention. "I should have told you I had Junie's magic."

"I agree," Andie replied curtly.

"I want to give it to you, but I'm not sure that you're ready for it."

Andie opened her mouth to likely argue, but Beatrix raised a finger and continued. "I'm also aware that it's your choice to make. Junie might have been my best friend, but she was your blood. If you're willing to risk the side effects, then we can do the transfer of power today."

"What side effects?" I asked before Andie could.

There was a twinkle of mischief in Beatrix's eye. "Andie could explode from the overload of energy."

Andie gaped. "What?"

I took a step toward the witch, but she laughed. "Too soon for jokes? I was only kidding. You might end up in bed for several days from body aches and nausea. You could have problems with your sight. Oh, and there's the chance your body will reject the magic altogether. If that happens, then the power would be lost, and you'll never reach the potential you could have if we'd waited until you'd gotten your birthright magic back first."

Andie's face was ashen, and I stepped back to her side, grabbing her hand. "How high is the probability that any of those things might happen?"

"Body aches and nausea is pretty much guaranteed to

happen. Vision issues? Maybe a fifty-fifty chance," Beatrix answered.

"And the possibility that my body will reject the transfer?" Andie asked.

"Slim, but how slim depends on how determined you are for this to work. You have to truly want this magic. By wanting the magic, you're accepting that you're a witch, that you belong within this coven, and that you understand all of the risks associated with that. If there is any hesitation within you, the energy will know."

I glanced down at Andie, wondering if she was truly ready to accept all of that after only returning two days ago. The tension she carried within the coven had disappeared after only minutes at the pack. Was it selfish of me to hope she was ready just so we could have a proper bond? Possibly. At the same time, I wouldn't risk her happiness in the long term and ask her to do this if she wasn't certain about what she wanted.

We'll support whatever decision she makes. We can't force her into anything she's not ready for and risk her getting hurt, my wolf said.

Agreed.

Beatrix raised a pointed brow at Andie. "So, how does that make you feel?"

"I'm ready. I understand what it means to receive this magic and I'm not afraid," Andie said with absolute conviction.

I turned her toward me. "Are you sure?"

She nodded, a glint of determination in her azure eyes. "Positive." She turned back to Beatrix. "How do we make this happen?"

Beatrix tried to hide a smile, but I could see she was just

as proud as I was that Andie seemed so certain. "I need to go to the Spell House for a few things and then we can complete the transfer after."

"The Spell House? What's that?" Andie asked.

"An offsite location where I do my business deals and keep things that not all members of the coven need access to. It's especially helpful to have separate from unruly teenagers who don't understand the seriousness of some spells," Beatrix answered.

Andie laughed. "Sounds like I missed out on some fun times growing up."

Beatrix's grin widened. "And some severe punishments. Ask Charlie about the time I gave her a pig snout for a full twenty-four hours."

Beatrix was one twisted witch.

"If you want to come, you have an hour to get ready. I need to make a list of things and double-check for anything else I might need for tracking Moira." Beatrix turned to open up the shield, likely so I could walk through.

"Any word on her?" I asked.

Beatrix's lip lifted in a quiet snarl. "She's been sending threats, but nothing I'm afraid of. I have the strongest barriers around my homes. Though, the two of you staying at the pack might prove to be a problem once Andie has magic inside her. We'll have to figure something out before Holden gets his panties in a twist because his pack was attacked."

Andie sucked in a breath and looked up at me. "I hadn't thought about putting the wolves in danger when we went there."

I hadn't thought about that, either, but I was sure Holden

had. If he'd been concerned, I had no doubt that he would have said something.

"Like Beatrix said, we'll figure something out for the long term. You won't be locked up here forever."

She nodded, but the light I'd seen in her eyes earlier was dulling by the second.

24

ANDIE

Showered and dressed, I felt better than when we'd arrived at the coven, but there was still something missing within me that I'd found at the pack. I wasn't sure what it was exactly, but I hoped to find out.

Hearing Beatrix tell me that she would give me my aunt's power was a relief, but the consequences weren't something I was looking forward to. I also hated that there was a good chance I wasn't going to be able to leave the coven for some time.

Putting others at risk just so I could have an escape was too selfish. I couldn't allow myself to do that, but I did know that no matter how much my heart still loved Charlie, I needed my own space and clothes.

She was waiting in the living room for me with Foster, and she hadn't pushed for any information when we'd come back to the house. I'd been living on my own for a long time, so the current living situation was a lot for me.

With one last look in the mirror Charlie had in her bedroom, I double-checked that the band at the end of my long braid was secure. If we were going to be messing with magic, I wanted to keep my pink strands out of the way for the day.

My eyes were a vibrant blue this morning as they appraised the light-red blotches on my neck. Though they were barely visible, I smiled, knowing they were marks from when Foster had devoured me the night before.

Just the thought of how he'd worshiped me had my core clenching. With a shake of my shoulders, I stepped out of the room.

The house was quiet. Hopefully, Charlie and Foster hadn't been sitting there in awkward silence since I'd gone to take a shower.

Nobody was on the couches, so I turned for the kitchen. Charlie was standing at the coffee maker, dipping a tea bag into a cup. Not just any cup, but the one from my house that I'd been drinking from the night she'd found me.

"How did you…?" Words were lost on me when she handed me the cup.

"I went back to your house last night and grabbed whatever I could that was salvageable."

Hot tears filled my eyes, and my throat ached with emotion I didn't know how to contain.

"There are a few boxes over there." Charlie nodded toward the table. "Some of it might not mean anything, but I figured even dish towels might be worth saving after seeing your house torn apart."

I set my cup down and wrapped her in my arms. Fresh tears fell down my cheeks, and we held each other tightly.

"Thank you," I said. "Those don't seem like strong enough words, but going back there, getting what you could, that means the world to me."

She pulled back, a few tears in her own eyes. "I don't know what it's like to lose everything like you have, but I'm here for you anytime you want to talk. What you've been through on your own is more than anyone should have to go through. You're so strong for handling everything like you have."

My eyes cast down and I reached for the cup of tea again. I wasn't sure how to respond to her compliment. I didn't feel strong. Most days, I'd felt broken and empty. Just getting up, doing the same thing I'd done the day before with repetition was boring, but it was also safe.

Re-watching the same movies and shows ensured that I wouldn't be caught blindsided by a sadness I hadn't been prepared for. Living alone, working a job that should have been temporary, living away from the only place I'd ever known, all of it had helped me avoid dealing with the abandonment that I'd felt for most of my life.

Not remembering my dad, but knowing he'd existed. Aunt Junie never coming back. My mom dying.

Every moment had hit harder than the last. Every moment had made me feel incapable.

Yet when Charlie saw me, she thought I was strong for having survived. That was hard to fathom.

"Hey, what's going on in that head of yours?" Charlie asked.

I swiped at the steady flow of tears tracking down my cheeks. "It's just been a long few days." I forced a smile to my face. "I'm fine."

Charlie grabbed both of my shoulders and gave me a little shake. "No, you're not, and you don't have to be. Being strong doesn't mean being okay all the time. It means you're a survivor of tragic circumstances."

She gathered me into her arms, and I lost my shit all over again. My body shook, and I squeezed hard around Charlie's waist. My chin trembled and I stopped fighting the sadness I'd been trying to hide.

Being back here, knowing the way I'd left this place and why, it was a lot to process, but as my tears slowed, a feeling that maybe things would really be okay settled over me. At least, eventually they might be.

I reached for a napkin on the counter, wiping my face free of tears, then realized that the two of us weren't supposed to be alone.

"Where's Foster?" I asked.

"He's with Beatrix. She's giving him access to the coven. You walking away last night brought some things into perspective for her. She doesn't know how to express her feelings all the time, but Junie was her best friend, and she always missed you and your mother after you left. Helping you feels like a final gift she can give Junie. When you didn't come back all night, I could see the fear of failure in Beatrix's face."

Maybe I should have been apologizing to Beatrix as well. I was an adult, but I'd stormed out like a child. Though I wasn't exactly sorry I'd done it. I doubted that Foster and I would have ended up at the pack if I hadn't. Last night wasn't something I wanted to be sorry about. Especially not when the mere thought of Foster touching me had me feeling flushed.

"Whoa. Where'd you just go? Care to tell me what managed to wipe all that sadness from your face with just a thought?" Charlie asked with a wicked grin.

I had no doubt that my cheeks had turned a brighter-than-normal shade of pink. "Nothing. I'm just glad to be here."

Charlie smacked her hand on the counter. "Bullshit. You better spill before I magically lock Foster out of the house."

I narrowed my eyes. "You wouldn't."

"It's been well over a decade since we had girl time. Do you really want to find out?" she taunted.

No, I didn't.

"We went to the wolf territory last night," I said.

She rolled her hand in the air to indicate I should keep going.

"And Holden had a cabin set up for Foster to stay in. I might have stayed there with him."

Charlie covered her mouth in feigned shock. "Did you have sexual relations with the sexy wolf shifter, Andie Bishop?"

"I didn't have sex with him if that's what you're asking, but we also didn't merely sleep in the bed. Though not having sex was a nearly painful decision to make, I do appreciate Foster not letting things go too far too quickly."

She groaned. "Not only is your soulmate easy on the eyes, but he's also chivalrous? I kind of hate you right now for being so lucky."

"I guess after so many things going wrong in my life, something had to go right," I said with a shrug before taking another sip of hot tea.

Charlie sobered. "Hey, I didn't mean anything by that. I'm really happy for you. Don't let my teasing take away from the greatness of what's happening between the two of you."

"I know. Thank you, but what about you? There has to be

some greatness in your life, too." At least, I hoped so. Both of us couldn't have had shitty lives after our forced parting.

"You know, once I got over the fact that I might never again have a best friend, things got a little easier. My parents helped me a lot in those early years after everything, but it wasn't until I was ten and enrolled in advanced magic classes that I started to find my place."

"I still need to see them. I feel bad that I haven't yet," I said with a frown.

"Don't stress about that one bit. They completely understand that you have a lot to figure out right now and that there isn't much time to socialize."

"After I get over being sick from this transfer of power we're doing today, I want to go to their house. See more of the coven while we're at it."

Charlie's eyes widened. "You're going to accept Junie's magic even after what Beatrix said? Well, that's assuming she told you all of the potential side effects."

"She did, and I'm ready. I don't have any doubts about what I want. Even though this is overwhelming, having my memories given back with such unfathomable clarity has gone a long way in helping me cope with all this."

"Well, that's equally surprising and not at the same time. You never were afraid of much when we were little. It's nice to see that hasn't changed." Charlie grinned.

I wanted to correct her. I often felt afraid of anything that wasn't part of my normal routine, like work and mindless activities, but I also wanted her words to be true. So I let them be. Though the thought of work reminded me I still hadn't let them know I wasn't coming back.

"Do you have a phone I can borrow?" I asked.

She went to the table and grabbed one that was next to

the boxes. "Even better, I have a new one for you. Your old one was fried that first night from one of those witches, but one of our magic tech crew was able to transfer a majority of the data from your previous phone to this one."

I accepted the phone with a relieved sigh. "Thank you so much. I need to quit my job. Though I feel horrible because it's probably the worst time in the world to do so. My boss had just left to go out of town and bury her sister."

"Shit. That's rough. Maybe just send an email?" Charlie suggested. "It's not like you'll need them for references in the future."

"That's not a terrible idea." I pulled up the email app and had to log in again with all my info. After three tries, I finally got the password right and everything began to load.

Eighty-seven new emails later, thanks to marketing spam, I did a quick scroll through to make sure I hadn't missed anything new.

"Oh. There's one here from my boss already," I said, clicking to open it.

"Maybe she's pissed because she couldn't get a hold of you and fired you already," Charlie said.

As convenient as that would have been, I'd feel like utter shit if that were the case. I actually hadn't been scheduled to come into work until this morning.

The email loaded, and I dropped my jaw.

"Did she actually fire you?" Charlie asked.

"No. Well, sort of. She's closing the shop. Her sister who passed away? Apparently, she was rich and left everything to my boss. She told us not to open the store, effective today, and that we'd be receiving severance packages in the mail."

I hit *reply* and wrote out a quick note, thanking her for

the update and declining the severance package. I didn't feel right taking it when I'd intended to quit anyway.

A bit of the heaviness I'd been feeling lifted from my chest when I sent the email. I thought I'd be sad, but instead, I was ready to see what came next.

Foster chose that moment to walk through the door with Beatrix right behind him.

As Foster's eyes appraised every inch of me, burning my skin with just a look, I was reassured that regardless of how stressful all of this was, the thought of having never met him, or returning to the coven, was even worse.

25

FOSTER

Beatrix clapped her hands, sidestepping me. "Who's ready to play with magic and hopefully not die in the process?"

My wolf growled so deep inside me that I couldn't help but echo the sound out loud.

She makes it very hard to trust her with our mate, my wolf said.

Agreed, but Andie getting this magic will bring us one step closer to getting hers back from Moira while also hopefully killing the dark witch.

When Moira's dead, Andie won't be in danger anymore and we can give her the life she deserves.

We can and we will, I said with conviction before I closed the distance between Andie and me.

When my arm wrapped around her shoulders, her head leaned against me, soothing the annoyance Beatrix had caused.

Andie looked up at me. "Did she give you access to the coven?"

Before I could answer, Beatrix cut in. "I did, much to the other coven members' dismay. Remember that when you think I don't care about anything other than myself."

The pain in Beatrix's words was evident. I almost felt bad for continually fighting with the old witch, but a lot of it she had brought on herself.

Beatrix flicked her long, grey hair back. "Anyway, we need to go to Spell House. Is everyone ready?"

"Are you doing the transfer there or here?" Charlie asked.

"I first thought to do so here, but Spell House might be better since we have all the books and extra potions there in case something goes wrong."

"Do you anticipate something going wrong outside of the earlier warnings you gave us?" I asked. Beatrix holding back more information wouldn't have surprised me.

"No. Besides Andie feeling like garbage for a few days, this should be an easy process. Mostly because you have me leading the transfer."

It was getting easier to ignore her cockiness, but it was still exasperating.

"Let's get going then," Andie said, tucking a phone into her pocket. I was going to have to remember to keep mine on me more often, especially if I'd be splitting my time between the pack and here.

Beatrix led the way out of the house and the rest of us followed until she stopped abruptly. I nearly slammed into her back and had to take a couple of steps back with Andie at my side.

Beatrix looked at Andie. "The portal we had to take to your house was different from normal ones. We were trying to mask our magical presence, but there's already a connection between here and Spell House that makes it so we don't have to be as cautious."

The old witch actually explaining the differences instead of leaving those who didn't know in the dark surprised me, and Andie as well, based on the incredulous look on my mate's face.

Andie watched Beatrix intently and I observed Andie just as closely. Andie might have seemed lighter at the pack house, but there was an underlying curiosity that she had for the coven and magic that couldn't be denied.

Maybe this was why Andie was meant for me. I could be the escape she needed from the heaviness of her world. Being the last witch in her line would also cause some sort of target to be on her back, but with me at her side, she'd always have a partner watching out for those who couldn't be trusted.

The portal opened quickly, and Beatrix stepped through first, followed by Charlie, then us. We entered the living room. The first thing I noticed was all of the candles lit, thinking it was only a matter of time before the place burned down. Then I took in the different-colored walls, varying from shades of blue to green to dark red.

Witches were odd creatures. At least the older ones.

"How about a quick tour before we begin?" Beatrix offered.

I could sense the eagerness in Andie as she nodded in agreement.

"The house has four levels. This is the main one, and below us is a basement. We'll start there and see the kitchen on the way."

The living room we arrived in flowed right into the kitchen. The space was smaller than I'd expected but open, so it didn't feel enclosed while we walked through. Next to that was a long table where a handful of witches and warlocks looked up, mid-bite.

Two men and a few women were eating breakfast. The smell of bacon and eggs had my mouth watering. Eating was something I needed to do more of now that I wasn't busy searching for Andie every day.

"This is Andie and Foster. Don't mind us," Beatrix said before opening a door on the left.

She descended a set of old stairs. The basement was dank and heavy with magic, but other than that, unremarkable with its concrete floors and walls and wood beams that I assumed were only for structural support and not design.

"Does someone live here?" Andie asked, gagging a little when she spoke.

"A vampire did, but he's gone now. A little project of mine that worked out quite nicely." The glint in Beatrix's eyes told me that she'd *enjoyed* her guest more than he had enjoyed being there. It wasn't often I felt bad for bloodsuckers, but in this instance, I did.

"Come now. There's more upstairs," Beatrix said. Charlie was already halfway up the stairs.

When we re-entered the kitchen, she shivered. "I always hated that basement."

"Maybe you shouldn't have messed with magic you had no business sticking your nose in. Then you wouldn't have become so acquainted with it." Beatrix snickered.

That must have been one of the punishments Beatrix had mentioned before. Twisted freaking witch.

Beatrix snapped her fingers and pointed ahead. "Come on. We don't have all day."

Andie shook her head, presumably at Beatrix's

snarkiness, but she tugged on my hand and we followed along without objection.

We left the kitchen and headed down a hallway. The walls were covered in dark wood that matched the floors and the three doors on our right were all closed.

"There are spaces nobody is permitted to enter unless you've been given specific permission to do so. We have various projects that are always happening. I assure you that you don't want to walk in on one at the wrong time."

Andie shuddered. "Something tells me I don't even want to come back to this house, let alone enter any of the rooms."

Charlie sighed. "That's a good instinct. One I wish I would have had when I was younger."

We ended up at another set of stairs, these ones headed to the second floor. Beatrix went up without waiting and the three of us walked a few steps behind her.

We got to the next floor and the wood floors creaked beneath my feet. There was an open area just ten feet past the stairs with cabinets on the wall and an empty counter.

Beatrix began opening drawers and pulling items out. Some were liquid, while others looked like seasonings you'd cook with.

"I guess the tour is over," Andie said.

"I'll show you the rest before we get started," Charlie replied while Beatrix mumbled incoherently to herself, then cursed.

"Need any help?" Charlie offered.

Beatrix looked up. "Hmm, I guess. Go back downstairs and in the fridge, grab me a vial of vampire blood. That should quicken Andie's healing process from the transfer."

"Vampire blood?" Andie gaped.

I gave her hand a reassuring squeeze. "Without a

vampire's venom, their blood is typically only used for good things."

She gulped loudly. "Awesome. How about there be no other naming of ingredients to this spell?"

Beatrix snickered. "What fun would that be? We've got—"

I cut her off. "That's enough prodding for the moment, Beatrix."

"You two are no fun." She huffed, then went back to searching for whatever it was she needed.

Something about this place is different, my wolf said.

How so?

I don't know. When we entered the coven for the first time, there was a change in atmosphere, but this isn't the same. The magic here has a different presence, but I can't tell if that's a good thing or not.

"Is the shield around this house the same as the ones around the coven?" I asked Beatrix.

Her eyes peeked up at me. "Why?"

"My wolf says something is different here. I want to make sure that's because it's supposed to be and not because something is wrong."

Andie tensed at my side at the mention of something being wrong.

"This one is stronger because it's smaller and easier to control. Impressive that your beast can sense that," Beatrix replied.

I wanted to tell her that most of what my *beast* could do was impressive, but I knew my words would fall on deaf ears, so I didn't waste my breath.

The stairs groaned when multiple sets of footsteps came

up them. I turned around to see three familiar people, but I only remembered one of their names.

Benjamin was there with the two other witches I knew had been present when Andie had gone back to her house. He stayed back as the older women came closer.

"Hello, Andie," the eldest said.

"Hi, Evelyn. Are you and Ava here to help?" Andie didn't seem excited about that idea, and I wondered why.

Ava stepped forward, reaching a hand to grasp Andie's elbow. "I'm sorry about yesterday. I wasn't on board with the idea of going back to your house. When things went wrong, just as I'd imagined they would, it further fueled my anger and I took it out on you."

Andie's tension released. "It's okay. I appreciate your apology."

Speaking of… Benjamin was still in the corner. He likely hadn't come any closer because of me. I knew it would make Andie happy if I said sorry to the kid for the way I'd acted when he'd only been helping her.

"I'll be right back," I whispered in her ear.

Before she could question what I was doing, I approached the teenage warlock. He straightened and flinched back a step when he saw me, his freckled face paling.

"Easy, kid. I'm not going to hurt you," I said.

He nodded but stayed silent.

I stopped a few feet from him. "I wanted to thank you for helping Andie yesterday and, more importantly, apologize for how I acted."

I didn't think it was possible, but his face got fainter. "Seriously?"

"Yes. Seriously. Andie told me what you did, and I

shouldn't have taken out my stress on you when you weren't the problem."

Benjamin let out a heavy breath. "Well, thanks, man. I appreciate that. I thought you were going to rip my head off if I got too close again."

I placed my hand on Benjamin's shoulder. "A piece of advice if you're going to survive this world. Always be the toughest man in the room. Even if you're not, believing you are just might save your life or someone else's one day."

The kid nodded, his red curls bobbing haphazardly as he did so.

"Come on." I gestured toward the others and headed back to Andie's side.

She was grinning at me, and I knew I'd made the right choice. Not only because it had been the right thing to do, but because Andie's smile had me standing taller.

26

ANDIE

atching Foster go apologize to Benjamin had been enlightening. Foster was an enigma that I was eager to figure out. I never knew when he was going to go all alpha or when he was going to keep his cool. I would have thought that was a bad thing, but as we interacted more, I noticed that even when he lost his temper, he was still very much in control. So I considered his unpredictability to be a good trait.

Charlie came back with the vampire blood, and I wanted to vomit. My skin crawled when I saw the crimson liquid slosh around the clear vial.

"A present from my new friends when I decided not to use them for tracking you," Beatrix said. She handed the blood to Evelyn. "Will you and Ava double-check all of the ingredients?"

"Of course, Beatrix." Evelyn grasped the blood vial and began poking around at all the items lying on the counter.

"Andie, I'd like you to come with me," Beatrix said, grabbing my hand without waiting for an answer.

I glanced back at Foster and shrugged when he narrowed his eyes on Beatrix's retreating form. We went down a hallway up ahead, and there were more closed doors. She opened one of them and then moved aside.

The energy of the room moved over me along with a floral scent that I remembered Aunt Junie always smelling like, and I shuddered at the familiarity. My throat pricked with emotion, and I glanced around, taking a step inside. The room had light-pink walls, nearly the same color as my hair, a twin-sized bed with white bedding, and a small dresser.

On top of the dresser was a music box I remembered vividly. My steps slowed and I lifted my hands hesitantly. The painted tin was just as I remembered. A vibrant blue with a moon on the top and stars covering the sides of the circular shape. I lifted the bronze latch carefully and raised the lid.

My fingers shook, and my eyes filled with tears, but there was nothing sad inside me. My stomach fluttered with memories of the past while the familiar, soft melody echoed from the tiny box.

I closed my eyes and swayed to the memorable tune. "Aunt Junie would bring this box with her when she visited sometimes. We would stay up past my bedtime and lie under the stars. She would always point to the North Star and tell me that whenever I missed her to look for that one. That no matter how far apart we were, the stars would always connect us."

Beatrix's hand covered mine, and I opened my eyes to find her cheeks wet as well. "There will never be a day that goes by that I don't miss her."

My arms wrapped around Beatrix's waist, and I hugged

her tightly. "She was lucky to have someone who cared so much about her."

Beatrix pulled back, laughing and wiping away the evidence of her feelings. "*I* was the lucky one. She was the only witch to ever put up with my shit."

"Aunt Junie had the best heart," I said softly, closing the lid of the music box.

"Now *you'll* have her heart. As soon as we get your house sorted, you can take this home with you. Everything in here belongs to you."

"Thank you, Beatrix."

She nodded stiffly and backed up a step. "We need to go into the attic with the others to complete the transfer. Are you sure you're ready?"

"I am." My words were strong and true. I meant them even more after seeing this room, smelling my aunt's perfume, and hearing the music box.

I settled my hand over the trinket and closed my eyes once more. *I'm going to make you proud, Aunt Junie.*

My chest warmed, and goosebumps rose over my skin.

"Thank you," I whispered before following Beatrix back to the others.

Foster was staring down the short hallway once we joined up with him again. Concern was etched over his perfect face, and I went to his waiting arms.

"Are you okay?" he asked.

"Better than okay."

"There was a whole lot of emotion coming from the direction you went."

I glanced up at him, smiling. "All good things. I promise. I'll show you before we leave."

He nodded, pressing me closer to him.

"Everything check out?" Beatrix asked Evelyn.

"Perfect as usual," the other witch answered.

Beatrix met my confused stare. "Even the coven leader isn't exempt from the rule of always having your spells confirmed by another witch. In this case, I asked both Evelyn and Ava to make sure I wasn't missing anything. This needs to go perfectly."

Ava patted her arm. "And it will. Upstairs?"

Beatrix nodded, then rubbed her hands together. "You two might want to back up."

Foster and I joined Charlie and Benjamin where they stood against the far wall. I watched streams of silver magic leave Beatrix's palms and rise to the ceiling, creating a square shape before the drywall disappeared.

Another set of stairs unfolded, settling onto the floor with a soft *thud*.

"Holy shit," I muttered, more impressed than I'd expected to be.

Beatrix went up first, carrying a box full of spell ingredients with her. Same with Evelyn and Ava. The rest of us, including Benjamin, followed after them.

Of course, there were no railings on the stairs to help me keep my balance, though. I didn't lift my foot high enough halfway up and kicked one of the steps. The impact made me sway, and I thought for sure I was going to fall the four feet back to the floor, taking at least one person down with me, but Foster was right behind me.

His hands gripped my hips, keeping me upright until I got my bearings back.

"Thanks," I said.

"You really are accident-prone." Charlie chuckled from below.

"Yeah. Well, at least I never had a pig snout on my face," I replied with a smirk.

"Low blow," she grumbled while we continued up.

Foster's hands hovered next to my sides until we got to the top, which had me grinning even more.

Beatrix was searching the shelves full of old books while I glanced around. They spanned the length of both sides to the room, filled end-to-end with books. At the front of the area, there were windows overlooking the yard, and at the opposite end of the attic the wall slanted down sharply, creating an unusable space.

The wood floor planks up here were cracked and spaced apart nearly an inch, but they didn't make a sound when I walked over them, so I felt moderately safe moving around.

There was a round table with a black cauldron in the middle of it. I smirked at the thought that these witches used something seen so commonly in fiction, but I also noticed there was no fire needed to cause whatever was inside to emit a fog-like substance.

"I shouldn't be here," Foster said quietly in my ear.

I whipped my head toward him. "Why?"

"Beatrix just made a very loud statement by bringing me up here. From what I know, not even witches outside of the coven are supposed to enter a spell room. This place contains centuries of old magic within those books."

Charlie stepped in front of us. "He's right. This is Beatrix's way of accepting Foster as part of you. The coven will be talking about this for weeks."

"How will they even know?" I asked, trying not to let my panic show at the thought that people would be gossiping about us. Okay, they were probably going to either way, but this made news of us even bigger.

"Those witches we saw down there? They'll know now that things are too quiet on the second level," Charlie answered.

Great. Hopefully, that didn't create any backlash for Beatrix. We were just getting to a good place. I didn't want to go backward with her.

"Andie, come sit in this chair," Beatrix said.

"What chair?" I asked when I turned around.

She snapped her fingers. "That one."

I blinked and there was a cushioned stool with wooden legs. I took a step forward, but Foster grabbed my hand, pulling me back toward him.

He had me wrapped in his arms in the next second, and I hugged him tightly back. I knew he was nervous, but there wasn't a part of me that was. I hoped that him not being able to sense a freak-out from me would help him cope.

His hands cupped my cheeks when he pulled back. "Don't be afraid to ask them to stop if something doesn't feel right. You're in control of what happens here."

I wanted to believe him, but I had a feeling that once things got started, there was no backing out.

"Everything is going to be fine," I said with conviction.

"It has to be," he murmured against my lips before brushing his against them.

Foster released me, but Charlie was next in line. She squeezed me nearly as hard as Foster had. "These are the best witches in our coven. You're in good hands. Just stay positive."

"I will. I promise," I replied, then I headed for the stool before Beatrix got snippy with me.

I sat down, my feet barely reaching the floor, and positioned myself away from the cauldron. I didn't want to see everything they were putting in there. That was when I would start to freak out. Hell, I didn't even want to know what was going to happen.

The *how* didn't matter to me, just the end result of having my aunt's magic. Knowing a piece of her would be a part of me was enough to make everything else fade away. Those thoughts made me think of something else even more important.

"What about my mother's magic that Aunt Junie took after we left?" I asked without looking back.

Beatrix returned from the shelves with a book in hand. "That was merged with Junie's when your aunt received it."

"So, I'll be getting both of theirs?" I pressed.

She shrugged. "I guess you can think of it that way, but Aspen's family line wasn't as strong as Junie's, so while your mother's magic is in there somewhere, you won't be able to differentiate it from your aunt's."

My lips tugged down. That wasn't what I hoped to hear, but at least a small part of my mother would be given back to me.

"We're going to start, unless you have any questions," Beatrix said, tapping her foot on the wood floor.

"I'm just supposed to sit here, right?" I asked.

"Yep. Sit there and look pained."

I glared at her. "That's not how the saying goes."

She winked before turning to join the others. "It is today."

Evil, evil, witch.

I swiveled around to see Beatrix and Evelyn holding the handle of the cauldron while Ava steadied the bottom. They walked together and set the pot down in front of me.

I peeked inside, then regretted my actions when bile rose

up my throat. I was pretty sure I saw some sort of small animal's feet and the liquid was crimson like the vampire's blood I'd already seen.

I hoped they didn't intend on asking me to drink whatever that was, because I was tapping out right then if so.

Ava began putting candles around us with clear crystals evenly spaced between them, creating a large circle that Foster, Charlie, and Benjamin weren't included in.

Cowardly, I avoided Foster's face, not wanting to see his concern.

"You need to put your feet in the cauldron, Andie," Beatrix said, slowly moving it closer to me.

My head shook rapidly. "Hard pass."

She bent down, yanking my Converse from my feet, and my socks went with them. "It's this or no magic. Just pretend you're at the spa doing something girly while a bunch of people watch you and hope you don't die."

"*Beatrix*," Foster growled in warning.

She waved a hand in the air without looking back at him. "Andie knows I'm kidding."

Mostly. I *mostly* knew.

Beatrix leaned over and checked the pot. "So, we're going to use the power of three for this spell. Normally, I wouldn't worry so much, but you don't have enough of your own magic to be helpful. You'll keep your feet in the cauldron, we'll say the spell, some other stuff will happen, and in eight or so minutes, you'll have enough magic inside you to maybe one day be a threat."

I nodded. "Eight minutes. I can handle that."

She met my gaze. "Yes, you can."

Dr. Jekyll and freaking Mr. Hyde.

Before putting my feet in the disgusting potion the witches had concocted, I finally looked over at Foster, Charlie, and Benjamin.

The latter seemed about ready to piss his pants. Charlie was giving me two thumbs-ups and grinning from ear to ear. I knew she was mostly excited to have her best friend back, and I could understand that. After my earlier meltdown, I was ready to be her equal and properly catch up after all our lost time.

Foster was doing his best not to glower. I gave him credit for trying, but there was no missing the tense set of his jaw, his thinned lips, and the storm brewing in his dark gaze. I knew that if anything went wrong, Foster would burn this house down without a second thought.

That knowledge shouldn't have made me giddy, but damn, it was something so surreal to know a man cared that much about me.

He nodded at me and tried to smile, but his lips barely lifted into a straight line.

"It's going to be okay," I mouthed, then I put my attention back on the three witches circling me.

Beatrix, Evelyn, and Ava were gripping each other's hands, keeping a tight circle around me.

"*Casteous radiumis,*" Beatrix said sternly.

The candle flames flickered and swayed. A silvery shield grew from the floor, rising toward the ceiling before curving and creating a dome around us.

I glanced back at the others. I could see Foster yelling at Charlie, but I couldn't hear him.

"No distractions. You need to be fully focused on this spell, Andie. Do you understand?" Beatrix asked.

"I do."

"Good. Now, put your feet in the bowl. I won't ask again."

I bent over and jerked my pant legs up as high as they would go, then did as Beatrix demanded. I gagged and covered my mouth when my toes entered the warm, thick and slushy mush, brushing against hard objects I tried to pretend weren't the little animal feet I'd seen.

"So dramatic," Beatrix muttered.

I glared at her. "I wonder where I got that trait from. I had five years to learn from you."

She smirked. The look did nothing to appease my growing unease.

With my feet fully submerged in the cauldron, the three witches began to walk sideways, keeping their hands out and palms only a couple of inches apart while they circled me.

They chanted, "*Incidium partacous sempera triperius defectum magaeous translatius.*" Each word sounded more jumbled than the last. They repeated them over and over while they moved slowly around me, but their speed increased when they started to speak faster. As their unfamiliar words began to slur together, a heaviness settled over my skin.

My muscles wouldn't respond to my movements, and whatever was in the cauldron began to smoke. I wanted to cough when the fog covered me, but even that movement was impossible.

I closed my eyes, submitting to whatever was happening. White lights danced in the darkness of my mind.

Just when I thought this wasn't as bad as Beatrix had made things sound, my spine stiffened and my head jerked back until I was forced to look up, but my eyes were shut tight.

I couldn't see the room, but abstract images pulsed inside my mind, blinding me with their intensity. I tried to turn away, but there was no escaping whatever was happening.

You're not alone, my little dragon, a voice whispered in my mind.

I choked on a sob. *Aunt Junie?*

I'm right here, but I need you to focus on the magic. Don't let it escape.

With renewed determination, I did as she requested. Instead of trying to turn away from the bright lights, I tried to get closer to them, drawing them nearer until the sight of them was burning my eyes.

The colors began to mix together, swirling until they became a funnel that dripped small droplets of colorful rain.

Call them toward you. Drink them in, Aunt Junie encouraged.

I did as she said and swallowed the magic, my throat bobbing when more of the churning paints continued to leak from the funnel they'd been forced into.

That's it, little dragon. You're doing incredible.

I wanted to ask her so many questions, but I was afraid to screw something up. Instead, I hoped that when things were more settled and I had some time alone, that I'd be able to call her presence to me and get some of the answers I'd been longing for.

Several minutes later, the funnel was half its original size, and my chair began to wobble. I still couldn't move most of my muscles and nearly toppled off the stool.

What's happening? I asked, hoping Aunt Junie would answer.

Drink faster, Andie.

That wasn't the response I was hoping for, but I did as she said. The drips turned into a stream, and I found it hard to breathe from the continuous gulps I had to take in.

Shouts sounded outside my mind, but I couldn't decipher what they were yelling about. All I knew was a heat was growing inside me and I was damn near choking from the magic I was inhaling.

I tried to slow the flow down, but the harder I mentally begged for it to stop, the quicker the energy was shoved down my throat.

A fire ignited in the pit of my stomach, flames licking up my spine, and I stayed frozen to the chair.

You're almost there, Aunt Junie cooed, but I could hear an underlying stress she was trying to hide.

The ground shook again, this time harder. More people yelled, and I swore I heard something about an attack.

I have to stop and help them, I said.

If you stop now, you'll lose my magic for good. You have to push through, little dragon.

What the shit is happening out there? I asked, but the question was more to myself since I didn't expect Aunt Junie to have any clue.

Language, Andie, Aunt Junie said with clear reproach.

I wanted to laugh at her response, but the magic I was attempting to inhale opened its floodgates and forcefully slammed into me.

I gasped for breath, trying to take everything it was giving, but my body shook just as hard as the floor beneath me. My insides ached with a fierceness, and the heat flickering within me grew to unbearable levels.

I'm going to die, I thought.

No, you're not. I won't let that happen.

I wanted to believe Aunt Junie, but my agony grew with every passing second, and any faith that I was going to survive whatever was coming diminished immensely.

Damn that devious witch and her powerful shields.

My fists pounded against the transparent barrier, burning my hands and forearms. Andie was shaking uncontrollably on the chair and the mist hovering over her seemed to be drowning my mate.

It's Junie's magic. They need to finish before they're interrupted, my wolf said.

Who the hell is going to interrupt them?

Just as soon as I'd asked the question, a hole blasted through the floor behind us. Charlie and Benjamin turned around at the same time I did, both with their hands out and ready to fight.

Except it wasn't an enemy who'd popped through the gaping hole. It was one of the warlocks we'd seen in the kitchen. Confusion at his dramatic entrance rolled through me until I realized that at some point, Beatrix had closed up the stairs. Not everyone must have access to this area which made sense given what was up here.

He rubbed a hand over his shaved head, and his umber eyes scanned the room. "Are they almost done?"

"Why?" Charlie asked.

"Moira's witches are here. They're trying to break through the barrier, and they're damn close to succeeding."

"Shit." Charlie turned back to Andie and the others but continued speaking to the newcomer. "Call all able teams. Get them here now. We need to reinforce the shield and buy Andie some time. She can't lose this magic."

I grabbed Charlie's wrist, forcing her to look at me. "Is this why Andie looks like she's having a seizure right now?"

"Beatrix should be able to feel someone trying to tamper with her magic around the house. She's likely speeding up the process."

"Why doesn't she just fucking stop before she kills my mate?" I snarled.

"Because if they don't finish the spell they started, then Andie will lose the only link she could have with her aunt."

Mother fucking hell.

We need to go downstairs and make sure nobody gets up here who doesn't belong, my wolf said.

I'm not leaving her.

They're going to need our help down there and you know it.

My ears pounded in time with the pressure I could now sense pressing in around us. I stared at Andie. She was helpless but fighting to finish what she'd asked for.

Her face was ashen and dark circles were growing under her eyes. Her upper body continued to flail, but somehow, she stayed locked to the stool with her feet still in that damned cauldron.

I ran a hand through my hair, gripping the back of my head painfully. I was getting too emotional, and I couldn't do that. I needed to be stronger for Andie. She needed a mate who would do whatever it took to keep her safe.

My pulse spiked, and I closed my eyes, considering the facts I knew. We were being attacked. Andie, Beatrix, Evelyn, and Ava were stuck in that spell until they finished. They needed the most protection, which meant I had to keep people away from this attic.

My wolf was right. I had to go downstairs and stop the incoming witches before they even stepped foot in the house.

I moved back to the barrier, holding my palm just over the shimmering shield, and spoke to Andie even though I was certain she couldn't hear me. "I'll be back for you."

When I turned around, Charlie was there. "I'm going with you," she said. "If we can't keep them out of this room, we're all as good as dead. Peter, the one who came to warn us, he's already gone to gather the teams, but we need to prepare in case they don't arrive in time."

I nodded at Benjamin, who didn't seem as freaked out as I expected him to be. "What about him?"

"Will you stay here and let them know that we've called in all available help and are doing our best to keep the shield intact?" Charlie asked the kid.

He nodded with confidence, keeping his stance tall. "Of course."

"Let's go then." I stepped toward the hole Peter had made and jumped down to the second level.

Charlie landed next to me, then lifted her arms. Soft, golden tendrils of magic escaped her palms and circled the hole before the drywall stitched back together.

"It's an illusion, but it will have to be good enough for now," she said, then ran for the stairs.

I followed her, my throat getting hoarse as I moved farther away from Andie.

This is the best way to keep her safe, my wolf reminded me.

He'd better hope he was right, because I wouldn't survive another loss. Especially not my mate. I'd rather be dead than live in a world without her.

When we got downstairs, the front door was open and we stepped outside. There was a dark mist surrounding the shield, and tiny, white fissures were appearing every few seconds.

The other four coven members we'd seen in the kitchen were spread out along the yard with their hands up and magic pulsing from them while they fought against whatever was trying to break through.

"I need to help them. You keep watch and yell if anything gets worse," Charlie said.

I nodded but didn't pay any attention to her when she took off. Instead, I called my wolf forward and shifted. The euphoric feeling I normally got when I transformed barely even touched the dread building in my gut.

More witches appeared on our right. Not ones I recognized, but they contained no dark magic that we could scent. My wolf and I watched the new arrivals join Charlie's group. There were now ten of them in total with their magic flowing freely, trying to prevent the shield from caving in, but when we looked up, the thin fissures in the barrier had already grown into cracks.

My wolf let out a short howl, and Charlie turned around. We looked up at the bigger fractures, and she followed our gaze.

"Damn it," Charlie muttered before shouting, "They're getting in whether we like it or not! Save your energy and regroup in front of the house. We need to keep them out at all costs."

Each of the other witches pulled their magic back to themselves and followed Charlie to where I stood.

Just when I considered shifting and directing some of them to the back side of the house, Charlie pointed at four of them herself. "We need people in the back. Hurry."

Three women and Peter followed her orders. Thunder cracked in the sky above, and I wondered briefly what the neighbors' thought was going on outside.

After the echoing bangs, the dark mist began seeping through the cracks of the shield, speeding up as it got closer to the ground. When the fog touched the grass, it spread, then lifted back into the air.

A dozen pillars formed in the yard before a gust of wind blew through. When the air cleared, the mist was replaced by twelve witches. Each of them wore black robes with hoods covering their faces. A shadowy mist blocked most of their facial features, except for the silver rings around their eyes.

Charlie fired off several orbs of magic back-to-back, triggering the other witches in her coven to do the same.

I stayed put, not wanting to get hit in the crossfire. I'd guard the door, preventing anyone from getting inside. Heads would roll before I let that happen.

We'll keep our mate safe, my wolf said in agreement.

The hooded witches flew across the yard, ramming into the ones on our side. Energy collided and sparks ignited around us, but even with all the chaos, my wolf eyes watched every movement that came near the porch.

A dark witch lifted their arms, but the loose robe they wore kept their hands covered. I couldn't tell what they were trying to do, and I wasn't going to wait around to find out. We lunged for the cloaked figure, teeth bared and ready for blood.

My wolf's jaw closed around the witch's neck, tightening until bones snapped and blood coated our tongue.

We gave the witch a solid shake before loosening our hold, enjoying the reverberating *thud* that sounded when the body hit the porch.

All at once, the other hooded witches screeched together.

"They're linked!" Charlie shouted.

Something about that knowledge was important, but I wasn't sure why. Regardless, we moved back to the door.

Charlie was joined by Peter, and they took another witch down. More screams echoed from within the shadows of the incoming witches, but I ignored them when I saw one of the good ones pinned down.

A war grew within me. If I moved too far from the door, then it made Andie and the others vulnerable, but if I didn't help, one of Andie's coven members could die. I didn't know this woman, and Andie might not know her, either, but something urged me to leap in and assist.

With a few quick glances, I made sure there weren't any close threats, then launched off the porch. My wolf rammed into the side of the cloaked witch, allowing the one on our side to get up.

She nodded at me with familiar amber eyes, but before I could think too much, I heard shouts from within the house.

Fuck! I knew we shouldn't have left. My wolf dug his claws into the yard before jumping over three fighting witches. Mid-leap, I shifted back to my human form, wanting my two feet to race up the stairs.

Commotion sounded in the kitchen, but that wasn't my

concern. Making sure my mate was still safe was all I cared about.

With only a few bounds up the steps, I was on the second floor and sagged in relief when the ceiling was still intact.

I moved forward to look around the corners and make sure no one was hiding. As I did, I glanced up, searching for the illusion that Charlie had created. While I was momentarily distracted, something slammed into my chest.

At first, the impact only pinched and made it hard to breathe. Then the pressure worsened, traveling from my chest down my stomach and to my legs.

The room wobbled, and I roared, trying to fight off whatever was weighing me down.

A woman with silver rings around black eyes loomed over me. "A wolf in a witch's spell house… I'd kill you, but Moira might find you interesting to play with. Be a good boy and stay."

She patted my head like I was a pet, and I was helpless to do anything. She disappeared back into the room she'd been hiding in before.

Can you fight this? I asked my wolf.

Too dark, he murmured.

A shimmer above me caught my attention, and I watched, waiting for Andie to appear. Except she wouldn't know there was someone waiting to attack, and I had no way to warn her.

The stairs descended from the ceiling, and Beatrix came down first, glowing silver hands held out in front of her. She saw me on the floor first and slowed her steps. "Is anyone up here?"

I couldn't even move my head to respond.

Beatrix rushed down and placed her hand over my chest. "You'll feel better in a few minutes."

Evelyn and Ava followed down the steps next, and a rumble vibrated through my chest.

"Andie's fine. Mostly. We have to help the others. I can't wait for you to feel better. Benjamin is up there with Andie. Use the hole to join them when you can walk. I need to hide the stairs again," Beatrix said, then she motioned for Evelyn and Ava to keep following her.

I made another rumbling noise, but the witches ignored my warning, disappearing downstairs.

The witch who'd hit me stepped back out with a grin on her face. "Don't you just love a good cloaking charm? Now it's time to have some fun."

She leapt into the air, disappearing through Charlie's illusion of a patch job, and a fire like I'd never known before ignited within me.

28

———

ANDIE

The funnel of magic was gone. Well, not gone exactly. I'd swallowed the whole damn thing while doing my best not to choke and die.

While I was pretty sure I'd survived, my body felt like death. Everything from my neck to my toes ached from muscles that felt like they were on fire and my head was thrumming with energy that prevented me from passing out like I wanted to.

I did it, Aunt Junie, I whispered.

I waited and waited for a response, but nothing came. Though in my heart, I could feel her presence and hoped I'd get to talk to her again soon. Hopefully, my mother as well.

Beatrix, Evelyn, and Ava had raced from the room after giving Benjamin instructions to watch over me. Though they hadn't said why, and I badly needed to know what was happening.

More importantly, why wasn't Foster here instead of Benjamin?

Benjamin picked me up from my slumped position on

the floor, next to the cauldron. Though, I didn't even remember getting off the stool. He carried me toward the wall with the windows and propped me up. Only, that didn't help all that much given I was struggling to hold my own head up.

"I'd try to help with magic, but it doesn't seem as if the spell went as planned. I don't want to make anything worse," Benjamin said, adjusting my head for me.

I groaned. "What's going on? Where're Foster and Charlie?"

My words sounded garbled to my ears, but Benjamin seemed to understand them.

"Charlie and Foster left first to make sure no witches who didn't belong got inside the house. Beatrix, Evelyn, and Ava just went to join them, but from the sounds of it, Charlie and Foster must be severely outnumbered."

I tried to listen for any signs that there was fighting in the house, but the thrumming inside my mind made it impossible to focus on anything that wasn't right in front of me.

Benjamin's head whipped around to stare behind us. "Someone's coming."

I struggled to move, not wanting to be a sitting duck if that someone wasn't friendly.

Benjamin stood in front of me, his knees slightly bent and hands out. He was just a kid. He shouldn't have been trying to protect me by himself, but as I was finally able to lean forward, his magic bit at the exposed skin on my forearms.

Just because he was a teenager didn't mean he wasn't strong, apparently.

With a groan of determination, I used every effort I had to position myself better. A pulsing sensation vibrated within me, and I wished Aunt Junie was still in my head to explain what I was supposed to do with this new energy.

A cloaked head rose up from the jagged opening in the floor, and silver-ringed eyes landed on me. She cackled, or at least I thought it was a woman from the high-pitched sound.

"They left a boy to protect their most prized witch. It's like taking candy from a child," the witch taunted.

A flurry of magic swirled like a tornado inside me, but I couldn't get anything to expel from my hands—not even my normal pink glow.

Benjamin seemed to have a handle on the situation, though. He shoved his arms out, and an invisible force powered through the room, sending the new arrival stumbling and tripping over her own feet until she landed on the ground.

Her hood fell back in the process to reveal ghost-white skin, black eyes within the silver rings I'd already noticed, and thin lips that tightened into a sneer.

She didn't bother to retaliate with words. Instead, a dark mist built around her, and she thrusted the energy toward Benjamin.

The fog covered him and extended far enough to touch my feet. The contact made my skin boil, and Benjamin screeched from within the cloud he was locked in.

I took a steadying breath, pulling my legs back before kicking them forward. My bare feet hit Benjamin's legs, tripping him and throwing him off-balance so that he tumbled outside of the poisonous mist.

He crawled farther away from the darkness, but that also put him farther away from me.

I continued to draw on the adrenaline that was building

inside me, hoping like hell my witchy instincts were going to kick in at any moment.

The dark witch sauntered toward me and extended her arms, revealing a dagger in one hand and an orb in the other. "How well you obey me decides which of these I get to use."

A familiar roar sounded from below, but I couldn't focus on Foster when my own life was minutes from being over.

I gritted my teeth and pressed my palms together. *Come on, magic. Do something.*

A light purple glow finally emitted from between my hands, and I pulled them apart just in time to shove one of them against the witch's chest.

She bellowed, moving several steps back, and her fist enclosed over the orb. Sparks of black flickered in the air before disappearing.

My chest was heaving from the effort that one hit took, telling me that I wasn't going to be prepared to fight back against whatever she had planned next.

The witch raised the silver blade and raced toward me again. I was working my legs up to my chest so I could attempt to kick her away from me, but they wouldn't comply. Everything inside me was weighed down from the spell Beatrix had performed on me.

I braced myself, trying to guess the witch's trajectory so I could at least attempt to roll out of the way and buy myself some more time.

Except as she made the final lunge for me, Benjamin threw himself between us. He blasted her with enough magic to send her crashing into one of the bookshelves, but I didn't pay enough attention to see if the witch was injured.

Instead, my eyes saw a dagger sticking out of Benjamin's

chest. His light-blue eyes were wide with fear, and his throat gargled for air.

One painful movement at a time, I forced myself to get closer to him. I was lying on my stomach and grabbed his hand. "It's okay, Benjamin. I'm going to get help."

Blood trickled from his mouth when he coughed, turning his head toward me. "Too late."

I shook my head. "No, it's not. I'm not going to let you die."

His lips attempted to lift. "It's okay, Andie."

I hit my free hand against the wood floor. "No, it's not, damn it!"

Benjamin *shushed* me with soft tones. He was comforting me. Yet *he* was the one dying.

I screamed for help, but when I looked up, there wasn't a friendly face in sight.

The witch was back.

She leaned forward and jerked the dagger out from Benjamin's chest, causing him to gasp and moan loudly.

"You're going to pay for his interference," she said to me.

"And you should have killed me when you had the chance," Foster's voice growled, then he roared once again, charging forward.

I watched Foster pick up the witch with ease and throw her into the opposite wall with a force I didn't think any man could be capable of.

The witch's body connected with the drywall and snapped two-by-fours before the momentum of Foster's throw ceased. The silver in her eyes faded, and her body hung lifelessly within the wall.

Hope filled my chest. Foster could get one of the healers. Benjamin would be okay. He didn't have to die protecting me. Except when my eyes fell on the kind boy's face again, his features were slack.

I gripped Benjamin's hand tighter, then looked up at the man who saved us. "Foster, please get help."

Foster's raging eyes softened in sympathy. "Andie…"

"No, don't say what you're thinking. He has to be okay." My eyes and throat burned while I tried to deny what was right in front of me.

Foster's warm hands covered my shaking shoulders. "I'm sorry, Andie. I should have been here."

Hot tears trailed down my face, but my sorrow was interrupted by a groan coming from the witch I'd been certain was dead.

Foster kneeled next to me, and we both stared at the smoke rising from the witch.

I flinched when her head snapped up. Her now-entirely-black eyes met my gaping stare.

"This is only the beginning, Andie. Surrender to me or continue to watch the people around you die. The choice is yours."

The witch's mouth never moved, but the sound had definitely come from her. My stomach churned with nausea.

Foster stood and took a step toward the witch, but in the next second, her body turned to ash, and she became nothing more than a pile on the floor to be swept up later.

Beatrix and Evelyn rushed into the room just moments too late. Evelyn gasped and joined me on the floor with Benjamin, her hands glowing a soft-white color. She pressed them over his chest, but I wasn't holding my breath for positive results.

"How did this happen?" Foster demanded before he picked me up from the ground.

"Moira," Beatrix answered. "I don't know how she knew we'd be here, but she's stronger than even I realized."

"No fucking shit," Foster spat. "We need to kill her before she even *thinks* to attack again."

Beatrix nodded, then looked at me. "We'll bring together as much original magic as we can and rain hellfire on the bitch."

"Let's do it," I said with conviction.

Moira had stolen my magic. Her witches had ruined my home. And what happened to Benjamin…they'd pay for dearly.

I might not have been raised in the world I belonged in, but Moira had just done me a favor. She'd awoken a fury inside me that would be all the motivation I needed to master whatever was inside me.

I would kill that witch for her selfishness, because losing another person in my life wasn't an option that I was willing to accept.

Want to know what happens next? Preorder Altered Magic today!
Want to chat all things Fated to the Wolf? Join my reader group Heather Renee's Book Warriors!

Also, a quick note, if you did not download the ebook version of this book from Amazon, or you were not gifted it directly from the author, then you are reading a pirated copy of this book. Please, delete this copy and grab one from Amazon so you can help support the creation of more books in the future! Thank you!

STAY IN TOUCH

Find Heather on Facebook:
Reader Group:
Want to talk all things books and get updates before anyone else? Come hang with me in my reader group!
Heather Renee's Book Warriors

Author Page:
Teaser and big updates are also posted here!
Heather Renee Author

Newsletter:
I send this out sporadically. Don't worry. You won't ever be spammed by me and you get a couple goodies when you sign up!
http://smarturl.it/HeatherReneeNL

ALSO BY HEATHER RENEE

Shifted Magic

An abandoned witch. A rogue wolf. Can the two save each other or will their bond only lead to destruction?

Scorned by Blood

A complete New Adult Vampire series featuring a not-so-human leading lady and the sexy vampire bound to protect her no matter the cost.

Luna Marked

A complete New Adult wolf shifter series (dual POV) featuring a strong-willed leading lady and a patient, yet fierce alpha male.

Broken Court

A complete New Adult Urban Fantasy series featuring an unconventional and anti-heroine leading lady, a broody love interest, and a fae kingdom with a vile king.

Royal Fae Guardians

A complete Young Adult Urban Fantasy series featuring fae, magic users, a sweet romance, along with snark and humor.

Shadow Veil Academy

A complete Upper Young Adult Urban Fantasy Academy series featuring shifters, elves, witches, and more.

Elite Supernatural Trackers

A complete New Adult Urban Fantasy series featuring witches, demons, a smart-mouthed female lead, alpha males, and a snarky fairy sidekick.

Raven Point Pack Series

A complete Upper Young Adult Paranormal Romance series featuring wolves, witches, vengeance, and fated mates.

Blood of the Sea Series

A complete Young Adult Paranormal Romance series featuring vampires, open seas adventures, and the occasional pirate.

Standalone

Marked Paradox - A complete Young Adult Fantasy fae story about a realm divided and one fae to bring them back together.

ABOUT THE AUTHOR

Heather Renee is a *USA Today* bestselling author who lives in Oregon. She writes urban fantasy and paranormal romance novels with a mixture of adventure, humor, and sass. Her love of reading eventually led to her passion for writing and giving the gift of escapism.

When Heather's not writing, she is spending time with her loving husband and beautiful daughter, going on their own adventures. For more ways to connect with her, visit www.HeatherReneeAuthor.com.